DEAD MEAT

ALSO BY BILL MUIR

VEGAN STRONG

&

THE ADVENTURES OF SERGEANT

PIGGY

DEAD MEAT

THE FUTURE OF FOOD IS KILLER

Bill Muir

SGT VEGAN PRESS

2022

ISBN: 9798841190875
Library of Congress Control Number: 2022913376

Cover Art & Layout: Andrew Gomez IV

Interior Layout: Bill Muir

Editor: Shawna Kenney

Photo of the author: Yasuo Uotate

SGT VEGAN PRESS
Los Angeles, California
www.sgtvegan.com

Printed in the United States of America

DEDICATION

This book is dedicated to animal

and human rights activists everywhere,

and to the worldwide vegan movement.

Finally, a shout out

to my brothers and sisters in the armed services.

Freedom isn't free.

ACKNOWLEDGEMENTS

The author would like to thank Hayden Fowler, Robert Garcia,

Todd Goldman, Dan Lysk, and Chris Tolentino

for their help with this project.

A special thanks to Rachel Murillo for her tireless support.

"First they came for the socialists,

and I did not speak out—

Because I was not a socialist.

Then they came for the trade unionists,

and I did not speak out—

Because I was not a trade unionist.

Then they came for the Jews,

and I did not speak out—

Because I was not a Jew.

Then they came for me—

and there was no one left to speak for me."

-Friedrich Gustav Emil Martin Niemöller

"Those who can make you believe absurdities can make

you commit atrocities."

-Voltaire

INTRO

John's LRS (Long-Range Surveillance) team was on patrol deep behind enemy lines. Their mission: to scout out enemy troop movements and to report back to headquarters. So far, no sign of the enemy, just a lot of trees in the middle of boring nowhere. John didn't mind, because he was having a good day. He had slept out under the stars and had eaten his favorite Meal, Ready-to- Eat, the dairy-free pizza rolls, for breakfast. He was doing a job he loved and often boasted to his family that he basically got paid to go camping with his best friends.

John was 5'10" with a medium build and brown hair he wore just long enough to be mistaken for a civilian when out of uniform. He turned to crack a joke to his buddy Mike. Mike was a tall, strong Texan with a wicked sense of humor. John and Mike had gone to basic training together and were closer than brothers.

John suddenly froze because he didn't know how to react. Just a minute ago Mike was laughing, and now Mike was missing his face. Smoke and fire were everywhere. John's ears rang with pain. His whole world was knocked out of focus. He could feel bullets whizzing by his head and see explosions all around him. He spat. Somehow, part of Mike's brain had made it into his mouth during the improvised explosive device (IED) blast.

The team had walked right into an ambush, and now they were surrounded by the enemy. John knew they were truly fucked but he refused to simply give up and die. It's not so much that he had a lot to live for. John didn't have a girl waiting for him back home, or any promising career or future. He didn't even have a bucket list. It was more a thing of stubbornness. John didn't want to give these assholes the satisfaction of taking his life.

John shook his head, coming to his senses. He knew if he didn't do something soon, he would certainly join his dead friends in the afterlife.

"Let's get these motherfuckers!" John yelled, and his MG 42 roared to life. The MG 42, short for MACHINE GUN 2042, was an AMERICAN 7.62 mm, air-cooled, belt (or magazine) fed, open bolt weapon capable of sufficient accuracy to engage area targets and vehicles at 2500 yards, or smaller specific targets like people at 2000 yards.

John sawed an enemy soldier in half with his first burst of gunfire. He watched the boy sputter around on the ground, crying for his mother in a language that John didn't speak. It was a sight that John had witnessed time and time again and he didn't need subtitles to understand it. John sensed movement out of the corner of his eye and jumped for cover. Bullets came smashing down on him but bounced harmlessly off the rocks. There were a few more shots, followed by a "click." John smiled. That was the sound he had been waiting for.

John looked out and spied the enemy soldier changing magazines. He stood up and calmly put the machine gun to his shoulder. The man fumbled with his magazine, the pressure getting to him. John slowly lined up his red dot sight with the enemy, so they became part of the same picture. He took a deep breath, remembering the old saying his squad leader had drilled into him. John mouthed the words "Slow is smooth, and smooth is fast," and exhaled. Just as the man finally came to his senses and locked the magazine in, John put a 5-shot burst into his chest. The man dropped to the ground like a sack of potatoes and his entrails splattered all over creation.

John ran over to check on the first member of his team. Smith was pretty banged up but was still breathing and had a pulse. Suddenly, enemy soldiers appeared out of nowhere and charged at them with a battle cry straight out of every cheesy war movie. John laughed at himself for flinching as he leveled the MG 42. In one squeeze of the trigger, he burnt the rest of the belt, leaving nothing but dead enemy soldiers and a pile of empty shell casings.

John quickly reloaded his machine gun and then spun the weapon to his back as he began to check Smith more thoroughly for injuries. Smith, a massive guy from Alabama, was nicknamed "Dump Truck" both because of the man's muscular frame and because of the frequency of his trips to the bathroom. John grunted as he tried to flip his friend over to check for injuries on the man's back. This movement woke Smith, who was only temporarily stunned by the IED blast. He smacked John's hand away and picked up his XVX 8 FURY Battle Rifle, rejoining the fight. Smith pulled back the charging handle on his weapon, chambered a 6.68 mm explosive-tipped round, and fired.

Headshot! Smith smiled despite the dire circumstances. Smith loved headshots; they were like scoring touchdowns.

John made his way over to Rollins, the team's squad leader. Rollins was a smart, tough-as-nails, hard-charging African American from Brooklyn, New York. Rollins' quick wit and courage under fire was the glue that had kept this team together through many of their scrapes in the past. Before John could render first aid, Rollins got up and started firing his battle rifle as well.

Apparently, the enemy decided they wanted to see their families again instead of dying here with these Rangers, because they retreated the way they had come. Rollins radioed into headquarters what had happened, and they were given an extraction point. They each had to carry one of their dead friends on their backs, because they had vowed to never leave a fallen comrade behind. John saw flashbacks of all the good times they had together as he carried Mike's lifeless body through miles of wilderness.

Back "home" at their forward operating base, John couldn't stop thinking about his buddy Mike. Mike had been blown to bits. One minute Mike was there, full of life, and the next minute Mike was dead. Mike, who had worked so hard to "Be all that he could be," had his young life ended just like that. It didn't seem fair.

When the deployment was over, Smith, Rollins, and John received medals and were paraded before the media outlets. John choked back tears at his friend's memorial service. Mike had been posthumously promoted to Sergeant. John stared at his dead friend's boots, rifle, and helmet. He couldn't shake his survivor guilt, and he couldn't stop thinking about Mike and the rest of his dead friends.

Apparently, Smith couldn't stop thinking about them either. One night back in the barracks John was awoken by the sound of rain. It was a peaceful, quiet sound, and felt like it had come to wash away all his sins. He listened to its gentle sound, letting it lull him back to sleep. He opened his eyes just for a moment to watch it dance on his windowsill. Suddenly he sat upright in bed. It was bone dry outside, yet he continued to hear rain. "What the hell?" he muttered and got out of bed. Then he looked up to the top bunk. His battle buddy Smith had slit his own throat, and the blood dripping from his wound onto the plastic mattress cover had sounded like the pitter-patter of rain on the rooftops.

John immediately applied pressure to Smith's neck wound. His friend lived – he hadn't cut the artery –but he wasn't the same after that. "Will any of us ever be the same again?" he asked himself out loud, in the present- day emptiness of his room back at his parent's house. So many lives lost, and the ones that weren't lost over there came back fucked up in the head. Couldn't sleep, couldn't eat, couldn't function, living in a daze.

When he finally returned home, he felt like a stranger in his own country. It's not that people were mean or disrespectful to veterans, it's that people were oblivious of their sacrifices and the hardships they had endured. It was almost as if they had fought for the freedom of people back home to ignore them. The irony was thick.

The nightmares never ended. John's dead friends haunted him whenever he slept. Sometimes they would swarm him like zombies, but usually they just surrounded him, staring at him with their rotting, vacant eyes, asking him why THEY were dead while HE was alive?! John could never answer them. He would just lie there in the darkness, unable to move, unable to speak, paralyzed with fear.

Sometimes John wished he had died overseas with his friends. At least then he could have died a hero, in combat, instead of surviving just to live like a forgotten loser. Luckily for John, his parents were nice enough to let him live back home with them in New England as he figured his life out. They worried about him and the hell he was going through.

Years later, John was diagnosed with PTSD. A doctor at the VA hospital explained to John everything that happens to you has an effect, whether it is getting ice cream or going to war. The doctor said the trauma John experienced had made it hard for John to function as a normal member of society. "No shit," John had answered. The doctor told him that he didn't like to be cursed at, and John told him to go fuck himself and stormed out.

CHAPTER 1

John felt the hot, oppressive rays of the sun beat down on him. The combination of his sweat and the heat made him feel as though he was trapped in a microwave, being cooked from the inside out. John looked up, staring directly into the swirling flames of the sun. It used to not be so bad, he thought

Climate Change had created two seasons: hot and REALLY FUCKING HOT. During the hot months it was usually 90 degrees Fahrenheit, but in the REALLY FUCKING HOT months it topped 150 degrees. It was so hot that a new part of the ever-shrinking forest spontaneously caught fire every week. The only exception was the sporadic cold fronts that brought heavy rains without warning. John considered himself lucky to be in New England; it was much worse in the rest of the country.

Most people didn't spend that much time outside, so they were able to ignore the obvious effects of climate change. John didn't have that luxury. Since getting out of the Army years ago, he had floated from job to job, unable to keep any form of meaningful employment. The only job that he could get was working outside on a construction crew.

Most of the construction jobs had already been taken over by machines at that point, giving companies the ability to build quicker and become more profitable than ever before. The few construction jobs remaining were either related to maintaining the machines, or the unskilled labor that picked up the trash and did the few, highly unsafe things that the machines couldn't do.

John's job was one of the latter. The working conditions were shit and he felt like he was literally killing himself to live. Still, given the current state of the economy, and what was going on politically in the United States, he knew that he should be grateful to have ANY job at that point.

His psychiatrist at the Veteran's Hospital had told him that his military-induced Post Traumatic Stress Disorder was responsible for his short temper and would probably make it hard for him to stay at any job long. He also informed John that, because EVERYONE had PTSD these days, the VA no longer considered PTSD to be a disability worth paying anyone for.

"What am I supposed to do?" asked John, desperately.

"Have you tried drugs – I mean "self- medicating? That's what everyone else does, and that seems to work for them," chuckled the doctor arrogantly. The doctor sighed and took off his glasses to clean them. "Come on, you signed up for this. What did you think was going to happen?" asked the doctor sarcastically.

John punched the doctor in the face a couple of times, knocking out a few teeth and giving the man a black eye. That bought John a month in a locked psych ward with a "danger to others" profile, a $5,000 fine that John was never going to be able to afford, and a behavioral flag on his VA record.

John didn't regret punching the doctor, but it DID make him realize he had anger issues. Since getting out of the Army he had noticed he certainly had developed an explosive temper. John would go from being just mildly annoyed to at his boiling point in a mere matter of seconds. Sometimes he felt as though he was white knuckling it just to make it through his day without exploding into a blind, atomic fury. This made him more likely to lash out at people, especially when threatened, and almost everything about life these days was a threat.

John looked up at the sun again, lost in thought. On his way to work he had stopped to watch some teenagers get beaten to death by Special Services Troopers. The Special Services (SS for short) were a paramilitary- like organization responsible for crushing any opposition to the government. They had very little oversight and answered only to the President himself. John felt bad for the kids, and wondered if the savage beating they received was warranted. He had wanted to intervene but knew that getting involved would have just gotten him killed, and his family rounded up and sent to the slaughterhouses. He also contemplated the crime which they were getting beaten for. They had spray painted in gigantic letters for all to see -

FUCK PRESIDENT WHITE.

John rubbed his temple. He had a headache, probably due to being dehydrated from working out in the hot sun all day long. No matter how much water he chugged he couldn't seem to shake it. His job had him removing broken pipes and trash from a construction site. The harder he worked the worse he felt. Still, he kept working, because he needed the job, and he didn't have any other prospects if he got fired. This job was his plan F, meaning plans A-E had already fallen through. He vowed that he would keep working until the day was over, or he dropped dead from heat exhaustion. Without a job, there would be no money, and with no money, there would be no way of ever being able to move out of his parent's house and get his own place.

John's boss was a fat, middle- aged man named Louie. Louie had given John a break when others hadn't, and John was grateful for the chance to redeem himself. That chance to make something of himself had made John into a loyal worker. He worked hard for Louie, and he fell into the same mode as when he was in the service. Do or die, victory or death.

John had just finished up his morning tasks and was getting ready for lunch when he heard the rumble of trucks pulling up to the construction site. He took off his hardhat and wiped the sweat off his face. When he opened his eyes, he could see that they were Special Services vehicles. Armed-to-the-teeth Troopers dressed all in black spilled out of the trucks and spread out in the construction site. When they approached the construction workers, the Troopers told the work crew to line up and demanded to see everyone's identification papers.

Louie immediately spoke up, flapping his arms wildly to get the Trooper's attention. John smirked, thinking that this gesture made Louie slightly resemble the animal that used to be called a "bird."

"What are you doing here? My guys are essential workers! This is a government contract!"

The Trooper-In-Charge (TIC) smiled from ear to ear. He loved his job, even though his job included rounding up innocent people and bringing them to slaughterhouses. Just the other day he shot a ten-year- old girl in the back for trying to run from the SS. If you asked him, this didn't make him a "bad" person. It made him a patriot.

"Government contract or no contract, I have my orders, and my orders specify to check EVERYONE'S identification papers, and that "EVERYONE" includes all of your workers as well."

The workers stood there in silence. The TIC continued: "After all, there is nothing more essential than meat, and by the looks of them perhaps some of these men would be better off being turned into food than to continue their miserable lives,"

The TIC laughed at his own joke, and some of his men joined in and laughed as well. John and his co-workers weren't laughing though. Anyone caught without their papers could be brought in and potentially sent to the slaughterhouses. While there was always the random chance of being searched and of something happening, people didn't worry about it. THAT was something that always happened to OTHER people. Never to them...but here they were, and NOW it was happening to THEM.

The Troopers checked the men's papers. One by one they were found to be in order and returned to the men. When they got to John, the TIC looked at his papers and whistled.

"HOLY-FUCKING-SHIT! We have ourselves a genuine WAR HERO! Exempt for life!"

To respond to the demand for meat in 2045 after all non-human animals had gone extinct, a program called "Project Carnivore" was established. Starting with prisoners (the first of the program's "volunteers"), the well-to-do were provided with choice, fine "steaks" made from inmates around the country. After they ran out of criminals and political dissidents, the homeless were next. Even the large number of the homeless couldn't keep up with the market demand, so the government needed to find a new way to fill that need.

All citizens were "encouraged" to make a tax- deductible "donation" of ten million dollars to the government. Those families that donated were given exemption from being selected to be part of the program. Those that couldn't –or wouldn't –pay were fair game to be "volunteered" to be turned into human meat. The only exception to this was military service. John's service had given everyone in his family exemption from Project Carnivore.

The TIC glared at John. "What the FUCK are you doing this job for, WAR HERO?! You should be out here busting skulls with us. Why the FUCK would you choose to do this shit job?"

John shrugged his shoulders. "I'm just not much of a joiner anymore, I guess."

The TIC looked again at John's papers and back at John. "Well, that's your right, so suit yourself."

The TIC moved to the next man, and held out his hand, waiting for the man to give him his papers. The man hesitated for a moment, stammered something, then shoved through the soldiers and started to run. One of the Troopers unslung his rifle and took it off safety. The Trooper brought the rifle up to his cheek, putting the running man in his sights. He was about to pull the trigger, when John's boss, Louie, stepped in his way.

"Please. Don't," pleaded Louie.

"Get THE FUCK out of my way," snarled the Trooper. Louie stood his ground though, moving from side to side to block the Trooper's shot.

There was a look of desperation in Louie's face. "Please, he is my sister's kid. I don't know why he is running. I just promised that I would take care of him. I'm sure that we can work this out. This is just a misunderstanding"

"I'm warning you, move out of the way or you'll be a dead man."

Louie didn't budge. Then the TIC casually stepped forward and shot Louie in the kneecap with his pistol. Louie let out a howl and blood seeped from the wound. Louie toppled to the ground, like a table missing three of its legs.

The TIC licked his lips and smiled. He looked around at all of the workers, and his fellow Troopers, savoring the moment. Then he shot Louie in the chest, and finally, through the head. He then signaled to the Trooper that was up on vehicle- mounted machine gun to shoot the fleeing man. The Trooper tracked the running man for a few seconds, then fired. A deafening roar came from the mounted minigun, spraying hot spent shell casings everywhere. They all watched in horror as the running man disappeared into a cloud of red mist.

The men stood frozen in fear. The Troopers had leveled their guns at all of them. Weapons were switched from safe to fire. There was an uncomfortable silence. Resistance was futile, and they all knew it.

John balled his fists. He saw red and he wanted to attack, but he knew that there was no chance of success against 30 men with guns. He steadied himself, took a deep breath, and finally said, "You didn't have to do that."

The TIC cackled and spat on Louie's bleeding body.

"Well, he shouldn't have tried to protect the kid. He not only lost his own life, but he also cost all of you sorry fuckers your jobs as well. Let that be a lesson to all of you! There is NO escape from the SPECIAL SERVICES. You are either with us or against us. There is NO in between! You've seen what happens to those who defy us."

The TIC pointed at John.

"Open your eyes, WAR HERO. Join the real men of the SS, or you'll end up dead like that plant-eating piece of shit."

The Troopers packed up and left as quickly as they had come. John went over to Louie. He was amazed to find that, while he was severely wounded, Louie somehow wasn't dead. John had one of the men call an ambulance, then tended to Louie's wounds the best he could. He put a tourniquet on Louie's leg and an improvised bandage to keep his brains in his head and held pressure on his chest wound until the medics arrived. John looked down at Louie as his life slipped away. Why had this good man been shot? What had brought their society to this? HOW THE FUCK was Louie even still alive?! Too many questions, not enough answers.

CHAPTER 2

John went with the ambulance to bring Louie to the hospital and didn't get home until late. To be seen at a hospital in the year 2050 required an upfront payment in cash, with armed guards promptly escorting anyone who couldn't pay for services outside. Louie's family had money and the doctors had done everything they could to save him. John had stayed with Louie's wife and their young child, watching the agonizing inevitable unfold until Louie had succumb to his wounds.

John was beside himself with grief. Louie had believed in him when others hadn't. Louie had given him a job when others wouldn't. Louie was a decent man in an indecent world, and he had paid the ultimate price for that decency. It had cost him his life, and now Louie's family was deeply in debt after paying his ICU bill.

John's mom and dad were relieved upon seeing John, but they were angry he didn't call. John explained what had happened. The news had reported things like this happening, but they were always to other people that the news made out to deserve it, like criminals, anarchists, and troublemakers. This was different.

As usual, John's sister Gloria was the first to speak. Gloria (or Ria, as her friends and family sometimes called her) was 21 years old, a senior in college, with shoulder-length hair and an athletic build from years of playing varsity soccer. Gloria was an intelligent and strong woman, and something of an activist at school. While John admired Gloria's dedication to fighting for a cause she believed in, he often worried her outspoken nature might someday get her in trouble.

"This is exactly why we need to rise up! When the people are united then they can never be divided," she said.

John smiled. Her optimism was contagious, even if it was a little naïve.

"Look," said John, "I love that sentiment and I want to make the world a better place, too, I just don't know what to do. People are literally dying in the streets, and others are being snatched out of their homes and eaten. I agree that we need to do SOMETHING, but they have the guns, and the numbers. Until there is an organized opposition, to speak out is crazy! It will only get you killed."

Their mother Maria and their father Rob nodded in agreement. Maria was 50 years old with long brown hair. She was considered skinny by most and the same weight since she was in high school, a fact which she took pride in. Rob was 55 years old, a big guy with a greying beard and in pretty good shape for his age as well. Sometimes him and John lifted weights together in a homemade gym in their basement.

Maria said, "I care about you both very much and if something was to happen to either of you, I wouldn't know what to do."

"Your mother is right," Rob added. "The government is insane. This is an insane time. We know something has to be done, we just don't want you to get hurt."

The TV box squawked to life with its nightly state propaganda. Every day at 08:00. 12:00, 16:00, and 20:00, a message was broadcast into every household in the country. TV ownership was mandatory, and people were required by law to watch every propaganda broadcast as well. TV viewership was monitored by the government, and there was a fine (and potentially much worse) for not watching the broadcasts. Still, because the internet had been outlawed and cable television cancelled, there was near perfect ratings during every broadcast. What were people going to do instead of watch TV anyway? Read a book?

President White was addressing the nation. He was dressed in a fine light blue suit and sported neon pink hair, as was the fashion among politicians in that age. His oratory style varied between loud and quiet, changing the volume and tone of his voice to emphasize the things that he felt necessary.

"Greetings to you, People of the greatest nation on earth. I, your PRESIDENT, am proud to say that we have once again MADE AMERICA SAFE by killing more CRIMINALS from the TERRORIST organization known as the Human Liberation Front (HLF). Here are some pictures of some of the TERRORISTS."

The screen flashed images of the mutilated corpses of people from all walks of life. Obviously, the point of this exercise was not only to brag, but also to intimidate, and the message was coming in loud and clear: mess with the government, and you'll wind up dead just like these people.

John noticed his boss, Louie, as one of the dead terrorists on TV. "Hey, that's my boss! That's Louie! How the FUCK did his picture wind up here?"

His mother scolded John for his language, and John apologized. "Sorry Mom. It's just that Louie never hurt anyone. He wasn't a terrorist; he was a big softie. He wouldn't hurt a fly...well, if flies still existed, that is.... He was killed trying to save his nephew."

The President continued, "America, when others could not keep you safe, I did. When others could not feed you, I gave you MEAT. I ask you to stand with me as we protect our great nation against the traitors known as the Human Liberation Front. Remember, we need to work TOGETHER to protect our nation from the forces of evil. In JESUS' name I pray that you all have a safe night. Amen."

The TV then switched to the normally scheduled program, the Project Carnivore Lottery. A lottery system to choose the "volunteers" was created years ago, and the "winners" were broadcast on live TV every night. Thousands of balls floated around in a big machine, and an attractive young lady read the volunteers' social security numbers live on the air. Those who refused to enroll in the drawing were tracked down and sent to the slaughterhouses. Those who ran knew their families will be rounded up and sent to the slaughterhouses instead of them.

When the broadcast was over, the family looked at each other. Once they were sure the government microphones were turned off Maria was the first to speak.

"Pardon my French, but that man is an ASSHOLE."

Everyone laughed. It was good to lift the mood, for everyone was down in the dumps. Rob and Maria told their children that they loved them very much, and John and Gloria said, "I love you," back. Rob commiserated with John about the loss of his job, and more importantly, the loss of Louie, who was a good man and didn't deserve to die.

Later, when their parents had gone to sleep, Gloria confessed to John that she had organized a demonstration at her school, to protest the systemic injustice inherent in the human meat industry. John was beside himself with worry, and almost screamed.

"ARE YOU FUCKING NUTS?! YOU'LL GET YOURSELF KILLED!!"

Gloria explained that she had permits for the demonstration, and that it was a school sanctioned activity. They would be within their legal rights to do it and would be sure to not step out of bounds. If the SS or the BRONZE (slang for the local police) showed up, they would show them their permits and quickly disperse.

"Besides," Gloria said, "If I get into trouble, I can always show them my exemption- courtesy of my big brother the WAR HERO."

"OK," said John, forcing a smile, "I just hope you know what you are doing."

"Trust me. What could possibly go wrong?"

"Oh fuck, don't ever say that. Respect the jinx. Goodnight."

With that, a shitty day ended. John went to sleep hoping the next day would be better.

CHAPTER 3

Gloria skipped her 10:00 AM Asian cultures class to attend the Human Agriculture protest. She had spent hours drawing and putting together the signs with catchy slogans and organizing the protest. The first sign featured pictures of people being killed, bearing the slogan "MEAT IS MURDER." The second sign, "DAIRY IS RAPE," showed smuggled photographs of women being raped at one of the local "dairy" farms. Finally, the last sign, 'BE KIND TO EVERY KIND," showed pictures of smiling children, because children made up a large portion of the human meat trade.

Gloria knew that a lot was on the line here, and that they needed to get more student support for the movement. While at least 20% of students self- identified as vegan, they still served human meat and human milk at the school cafeteria. As Gloria pointed out to her classmates, purchasing those products gave money to those who made innocent people suffer.

As she walked out into the quad, Gloria could already feel a menacing atmosphere in the air. Tension was brewing, and

THE STUDENT CARNIVORE UNION had showed up early to form a counter protest. She could almost smell the violence and hostility as the counter protesters shouted at them: "Go home hippies," and old standbys like "vegans taste great," and that "eating people is their right," and best of all, "If God didn't mean for us to eat people, then why did he make them out of meat?" She took a deep breath, exhaled, and walked up to the podium that had been set up in front of the stage. She could see lots of her friends in the crowd, but she could also see many enemies, and before she took the stage, she also noted the presence of the paramilitary unit known as the SS around the perimeter of the protest. She wondered how they got here so fast.

The SS had been called by the class president the minute he heard about the rally. While some free speech was still allowed on college campuses it was subject to approval by the governmental authorities. A division of the military, the SS still enforced many of the same laws that the police had, except that they themselves could not be held accountable for ANY of their actions.

When the country had erupted into chaos after the first food shortage of 2040, the president had declared martial law and put the country under military rule. The SS were known to be corrupt and in the pocket of Human Ag and the ruling elite. Sometimes they did humanitarian photo-op missions for TV, such as finding lost children and providing first aid to the elderly, but they were just as likely to sell the children and elderly to the butchers at Human Ag after the photo-op than to give them back to their families.

As Gloria took the stage and looked around, she counted over fifty SS Troopers in full battle gear, which was strange because there were only about thirty protesting students out there that day. She could see that the SS were armed to the teeth. They carried pistols, battle rifles, machine guns, and of course battle swords. Battle swords were perfect for crowd control situations because their battery-powered saw blades provided the operator with a 4-foot-long military- grade chainsaw that could be whipped into the crowd for destructive results. They were dressed in black from head to toe and wore helmets that gave them the appearance of skeleton warriors when their face shields were down.

The entire package was meant to intimidate, and the Troopers were indeed a scary sight to behold. Gloria steadied herself, believing that they were just trying to scare the students. She had a permit, after all, and her father had taught her to never back down from a fight.

Gloria stepped up to the microphone. She took a deep breath and drew strength from her friends in the crowd. She smiled when she saw the handmade signs declaring that the vegan revolution was at hand. She looked around and gestured for the audience to quiet down so she could speak.

"Friends, we are here to speak for the voiceless, so that their suffering can be heard. Human Agriculture is literally killing us. The writing is on the wall that its end is near. We protested when humans were killing animals. People then said they didn't care because humans were at the "top of the food chain." Now that all the animals are gone and there are only people left, they again try to justify murder, saying that it is ok because they aren't personally killing anyone. I say it is time for humans to stand in solidarity and declare an end to Human Agriculture, for we won't be free until all of us are free."

Gloria paused for applause, as she had done so many times before. She looked around at the crowd. The students were holding her signs and cheering "GO VEGAN! END HUMAN AGRICULTURE!" The counter protesters were moving closer to them, out of the sidelines where they were supposed to stay. The SS were also spreading out, moving among the students. This couldn't be good.

Gloria started to speak again but was cut off when one of the counter protestors suddenly shouted," Hey! He hit me!" and pointed at one of the students, who clearly hadn't raised a finger towards him and wasn't even facing in his direction. The student turned towards his accuser, who used this as an opportunity to strike the kid in the face. The student dropped like a brick. At the sound of a whistle the scene immediately descended into chaos.

Gloria stared in disbelief as violence suddenly and ferociously erupted all around her. The SS began indiscriminately firing into the crowd, killing scores of protesters outright and wounding dozens. A few of the counter protesters were also caught in the crossfire and joined the dead and dying students on the ground. Gloria saw several SS Troopers unsheathe battle-swords and chop off students' heads and limbs. The carnage was reminiscent of something one might see on a battlefield in the Middle Ages.

The remaining students held their hands in the air screaming, "Don't shoot, don't shoot, we aren't armed!" They were surrounded by the SS. The first two students were shot at point-blank range execution style - two shots in the chest and one in the head. Gloria could hear the soldiers laughing about it. The remaining students were handcuffed and left lying face down on the ground.

Gloria stood on the stage, her hands raised above her head, not knowing what to do. She wanted to run, but she feared being shot in the back. An SS Trooper climbed onto the stage to get her.

"You're under arrest for inciting a riot. Don't resist or I will shoot you."

Gloria kept her hands above her head and said "What do you mean riot?! This was a peaceful demonstration before you started shooting!"

Her words were stopped by a fist to the face. The Trooper's gloves were weighted, so it was the equivalent of being hit in the head with brass knuckles. Gloria saw stars and fell, but she didn't pass out – she was tougher than that. The Trooper quickly handcuffed her and left her on the ground. From where she was on the stage, she had a view of the cleanup. The news crew was there (late of course) and was taking a statement from one of the officers about how his brave men saved many lives that day when the crazy vegans attacked a counter protester without provocation. The SS officer who was speaking produced an obviously planted weapon from one of the dead students, demonstrating how dangerous the students really were.

After a while, two armored trucks with the words DEPARTMENT OF HUMAN AGRICULTURE in an arc with a smiley face underneath it pulled up. Gloria stared at the truck, knowing that the SS had obviously sold the students to Human Agriculture, even though by law they were supposed to be at least afforded sham trials before they were brought to the slaughterhouses.

"Hey motherfucker, I have an exemption! My brother is a veteran!" Gloria said to no one in particular. One of the SS Troopers climbed the stage. "I don't give a shit," he said, then kicked her hard in the stomach. He wound up to kick her in the face, when another Trooper yelled at him to stop.

"What's your problem?" The kicker snorted. "Going soft?"

"Nope. I just know that no one is going to pay money to fuck a dairy cow if you mess up her face."

'Good thinking," the other man said, and kicked her again in the stomach.

CHAPTER 4

The college kids were separated into three piles. The first pile consisted of the dead and the mortally wounded. In the second pile lay the living male students. In the last pile were the living female students. Both piles of the living were bound by their wrists and ankles. The students cried, yelled, and prayed. Some tried to close their eyes, with the mistaken hope that when they opened them, they might somehow awaken from this bad dream.

A skinny man with a receding hairline approached the male pile. He looked around, soaking in the scene, as if to savor the cries from the students and the sight of the dead bodies. He then smiled from ear to ear and identified himself as the Commander.

The Commander was a man in his sixties of normal height with a handlebar mustache. He was dressed in a black Class B SS uniform and seemed comfortable both in his clothes and in his position of power. There was nothing physically intimidating about this man at all, and yet there was a twinkle in his eye that made most people nervous.

He cleared his throat, and then addressed the male prisoners. "Look, you lot. You've probably already figured out that you are fucked, but there is a chance for you yet." He paused for emphasis, and then continued. "I'm prepared to let two of you live."

All the males turned to look at him, and then back and forth at each other. What did he mean, and was it a trick?

"I know what you are thinking, and no it's not a trick, though it would be a funny one if it was."

All the SS Troopers laughed.

"But no, seriously, I'm offering you the gift of life. So, who wants to live?"

The Commander looked at all the college kids lying on the ground. No one uttered a word, and for a moment Gloria thought that no one would. Then two of the boys started to yell that they would do it, pick them, that they wanted to live and would do "anything."

"Anything, huh," the Commander said with a sneer. "That's a bold lyric. Let's put that statement to the test, shall we? Free these boys!"

Soon both of the male students were freed. They stood in front of the Commander, shaking in utter terror as tears filled their eyes.

"Well, since you said you'd do anything to stay alive, I'm going to make you an offer you can't refuse! The offer to join the Special Services, to serve your country, to make something of yourself."

The boys looked at each other and then turned back to the Commander. The Commander produced two battle knives (the smaller cousin of the battle sword) and then turned them on. The boys watched, mesmerized by the glowing blades as they hummed malevolently. The Commander handed one of the blades to each of the boys.

"You're probably thinking that I'm going to ask you to fight each other, and the winner gets to become one of us. While I like where your heads are at, we've tried that before. It doesn't really work. Almost anyone will fight, even their own friends, if their life is threatened. That's not the test."

The boys once again looked at each other, this time in amazement.

"Now, it's not that we've gotten soft. No sir-ee bob, I don't want you to think that. I just don't want to take the chance of you hurting each other if you are both good candidates. That, and like I said, I didn't think that is as good of a test of the – er- qualities- that we are looking for here in the Special Services."

Another pause for emphasis.

"Ok! Very good! Do you boys know "Eeny Meeny?""
Both nodded yes. Pointing to the girls one by one, he counted:

> "Eeny, meeny, miny, moe,
> Catch a tiger by the toe.
> If she hollers, let him go,
> Eeny, meeny, miny, moe."

"Congratulations," He whispered to a short girl with blonde hair. "You have been chosen! Ok, here is the game! If you can stay away from this boy for 5 minutes, you get to live but he dies." To the first boy he said, "If she is alive after 5 minutes, we put you in a grinder and feed you to the other humans that we are fattening up before we kill them too. Begin!"

The boy chased after the girl, and the girl was able to keep away from him for at least 3 minutes, but then she tripped on a severed arm and came crashing to her knees. She turned around and back peddled away from the boy on the ground, doing what would have been called a "crab walk," in gym classes many years ago. The boy stumbled over to her, vibrating knife in hand, walking slowly and trembling in fear. The soldiers goaded him on, feeling their own blood lust rise.

"KILL, KILL, KILL", they chanted.

The boy finally reached her, and paused, raising the knife high. The girl screamed, pleading with the boy, whom she clearly knew. The boy fumbled with the knife, himself crying, a mixture of tears and snot running down his dirty face. Finally, the boy let out a scream, and stabbed her, again, and again and again, not stopping until her corpse was cut into pieces. The battle- knife made easy work through her body, slicing and slashing like it was going through a warm stick of margarine on a summer's day. He was, by this point, drenched in blood, and shaking all over.

"VERY GOOD!" barked the Commander with glee. "Now fuck her dead body."

The boy stood there, blood dripping from his knife. He wiped the blood from his face – more smearing it in then actually getting any of it off. "Sir?" he asked in a meek voice.

"VERY GOOD, I SAID. Now hurry up and HAVE SEXUAL INTERCOURSE with her corpse. What, is THIS where you draw the line?"

"No sir," the boy whimpered. He handed the knife to one of the soldiers and began to pull the dead girl's jeans off.

'STOP! You can stop now, you sick fuck. I wasn't being serious," laughed the Commander. "What's your name, boy?"

"Holden Park," replied the boy in a whisper. Holden was a small, skinny, shy, Korean- American boy. He was dressed in a way that made it easy for him to skateboard, which until now he had thought was the most important thing in the whole world.

"Very good, you've passed the test. You are now one of my dogs of war. Gilbert, brand him," he said, motioning to one of the skeleton warriors.

The man named Gilbert pulled a device out of his bag and approached the boy. He had the boy sit down, then gently cleaned the dirt and muck off the boy's face and rubbed an antiseptic jelly onto it. When the boy's face was properly prepped, he branded his forehead with the SS logo. Holden didn't move, even when the device seared his flesh. He was numb to life.

The Commander watched with a certain amount of satisfaction at the genius of this tattoo. Normally, Troopers were branded after they joined the SS, but it was only with a small, easily concealable tattoo of their individual blood type in their right inner armpits, which was helpful in the case of trauma. This, however, was completely different. For the rest of this boy's life everyone would know what he had done just by looking at him. There would be no covering this tattoo up. The tattoo also guaranteed that no one, neither the SS nor the HLF would ever trust him again.

"Very good! Now, moving right along, it's your turn," the Commander said, gesturing to the next youth.

Before the Commander could start in with his evil "Eeny Meeny" this youth went a different route. He leapt at one of the

SS Troopers and slashed him repeatedly with the battle knife. The Trooper fell mortally wounded and the youth grabbed his gun. Unfortunately for the boy, the other Troopers were fast to react and shot him before he was able to do anything productive with the gun. The Commander went over to the youth and pulled out an enormous blaster pistol and aimed it at the boy's head. Gloria let out a yelp as the Commander blew the youth's head clear off his shoulders.

"Well, that was fun. Let's mount up and go," said the Commander, and he whistled a merry tune as he walked over to his vehicle.

After the SS loaded up the trucks with the cargo – both the living and the dead- they drove through the empty streets. The first stop was the human slaughterhouses. Gloria recognized where they were by the smell. She had protested there many times, back when it was used as a place to kill cows and pigs. Now the industrial death camp had been retrofitted to kill humans and process human flesh.

After the bodies had been unloaded, the van's next stop was the DAIRY FARM. She also recognized this place by smell.

Not in her wildest nightmares did she ever think that she was going to be coming here as a "cow" herself.

The van doors opened, and the SS Troopers screamed for them to get out. One by one their leg shackles were taken off and they were lined up and then marched into the Dairy Farm. They were led into a big room and lined up. A woman dressed in a black uniform stood in front of them.

"Greetings, cows," the woman said with a smile.

"My name is Mother. You shall always call me this. The only answers I want to hear out of you are "Yes Mother" and "No Mother." Is that understood?"

In unison, the young women gave the right answer. One of them sobbed.

"There, there, little cow," the woman in black cackled. You are alive, and you will be well taken care of. You will be fed, given a place to stay, and a new name. Life was much harder on the outside. Life on the inside is much easier, you'll soon see."

The young women were taken into another room, stripped of their clothing, forced into showers and their hair shaved off them. Once they were completely clean, they were fitted with special cow helmets. The helmets made the women look like cows to some degree, at least masking their individual facial features. The main function of the helmet was to house a GPS tracker to keep track of inventory. The helmet locked in place around the girl's neck with a mechanism that was set to explode if the girl disobeyed orders or tried to escape.

After their helmets were locked on their heads, the "cows" were branded with identification numbers on their buttocks and led into yet another room. Men were allowed to select the cow of their choice and have their way with them. Because they were fresh "cows," the men paid a premium to rape and abuse them. Gloria cried herself to sleep, trying to block out the sounds of her friends being raped.

CHAPTER 5

Austin Youngblood stood staring at himself in the bathroom mirror. He had needed a hot shower to clear his head, so the mirror was foggy. He wiped the condensation off the mirror in a circular pattern to make his reflection clearer, and the squeaky sound made him smile. Then he took a good long look at himself. Austin stood 6'4", BLACK AND PROUD, with muscles courtesy of years of hard work and a beard that was finally coming in. Bad memories flooded his brain, and he stopped smiling. His reflection stared back at him accusingly, taunting him, asking him why he hadn't done more, asking him why he hadn't come to his senses sooner. He didn't have any reasons and he was out of excuses. He broke down crying on the bathroom floor.

Austin had worked for years as a police officer, a Bronze, a job he had once been very proud of. He had gotten his start as a young officer in the early 20's (now called the "roaring 20's, after the economic growth that had followed the first pandemic of the 21st century). He had fought against the criminals that had threatened his city, against corruption both in the police force and in city hall, and against white nationalist terrorist groups that had started to spring up all over the suburbs.

There was a time when he had felt that America had been moving into a "post- racial" existence. There had been a Black president, AND a Black vice president when he was growing up, and most of the top entertainers and athletes were people of color. Most people went to college, regardless of their race, and it looked like there would be prosperity for all. Even the minimum wage was raised, so people wouldn't have to work two jobs and still live in poverty. The roaring 20's had America on top of the world, and life was good.

Austin had learned in school that racism, classism, and xenophobia often came from a place of fear. Specifically, fear of losing, fear of missing out, and fear of being left behind. When there was a perception that others were getting ahead and taking things from you, that's when those fears were the greatest. As long as the economy prospered and there was the perception that there was enough to go around, people were happy and content, and those fears were kept in check. When the economy faltered, however, politicians were able to use those fears to get people riled up. They used race to stoke people's hate and play on their fears, and as a tool to divide the masses and to get them to vote against their own self-interests.

Talking to his parents as a kid, he had been astounded by their stories, and had been horrified by America's past. The fact that people of color – of HIS color- had once been bought and sold like livestock on the streets of American cities had seemed too impossible and too insane to be true. The fact that people up until recent memory still had to fight for the right to vote seemed crazy. And yet, it had happened. It was true. And as much as everyone spoke out against the evils of racism and talked about unity, he felt that the past was repeating itself once again.

When Project Carnivore first began, he knew that it was awful, but he had kept his mouth shut since times were tough and he couldn't afford to lose his job. After all, he had a family to think about. He kept his head down and kept doing what he had to do to make money for his family. Day in and day out he kept his mouth shut and his eyes closed and kept working. He did what he had to do, and he told his conscience to mind its own business.

Then, one day, everything changed. The day started normally like any other, with nothing out of the ordinary to warn of the horror to come. The weather was fair, and Austin was in a pretty good mood because he would be taking a much-needed vacation with his family in a couple of weeks. He was quite looking forward to it. He ate breakfast with his family, kissed them goodbye and then drove to work.

Once at the station the chief called him into his office and told him that his SWAT team had been called out for a drug bust. He prepared an operation order like any other routine mission, gave his team a mission briefing like he had done hundreds of times before, and he and his team readied their equipment and prepared to move out like they had always done.

When they arrived on location Austin was radioed by command and informed that their actual mission was to provide backup for the Special Services, who was there to raid an HLF hideout. The SWAT team took up positions on the rooftops, ready to shoot rebels and protect the Special Services Troopers as they smashed through the windows of the hideout.

The whole thing went smoothly until Austin realized that the HLF rebels were just kids, some as young as seven years old. Austin's daughter was that age and seeing that the so-called "enemy combatants" were just kids freaked him out. The SWAT team all lowered their weapons and watched as the SS Troopers led 20 small children out of building. The Troopers bound the kids' hands and legs and separated the children into piles of girls and boys. Then, in the distance, a small voice cried "Let my sister go," and shots were fired. In all the confusion it was hard to see what was going on. The SWAT Team Members watched as the Troopers opened up with automatic weapons, dumping magazine after magazine into the general direction where the shots had come from. When the smoke finally cleared, Austin could see the bullet-riddled remains of a small child lying mutilated in the dirt.

The Troopers gathered gleefully around the corpse. Austin could see them talking amongst themselves, and then they seemed to come to an agreement. Two Troopers each took an arm of the child and played a deranged version of tug-o-war while the other Troopers took bets on which arm would be pulled off first. After the Trooper on the right won, the next game was to see who could rip the child's head off using only his bare hands. A giant man stepped forward and was victorious. The other Troopers went mad with excitement, chanting his name repeatedly as the man held the child's bloody head aloft like a sporting trophy.

"ZEUS, ZEUS, ZEUS, ZEUS!"

Austin was sickened beyond belief. The blood, the carnage, and the cries from the little children shocked them all. One of his men vomited. Traumatized, the SWAT TEAM descended from the rooftops and watched as the Troopers loaded the crying children into unmarked vans. Austin approached the Trooper-In-Charge.

"What THE FUCK was that?" he asked

The Trooper-In-Charge looked surprised by the question and was perhaps taken aback by the language.

"What THE FUCK was WHAT?" he responded.

'Killing that child. You didn't need to kill him, but then to DISMEMBER him?!"

"Oh, that. Hmm, a little bit of harmless fun, I suppose." The Trooper-In-Charge looked at Austin.

"I'm guessing you don't approve. What, you don't like to play with your food?"

Austin was puzzled. "Play with your food?"

The Trooper-In-Charge laughed, and his fellow Troopers joined in the fun. When the laughs died down, the Trooper spoke again:

"What do you think we do with rebels?"

Austin stumbled with his words, so the Trooper helped him.

"Oh, come on! Where do you think veal comes from? Don't be so naïve…"

Then the Trooper-In-Charge changed direction.

"Anyway, thanks to you and your men for the backup. I will make sure to put you all up for some medals for the night's heroic actions."

Austin and his men watched as the Troopers got into their vans and drove away.

When he got home, Austin told his wife what had happened. He told her he knew in his heart that he should have done something. Instead, he did nothing except stand there and watch. He took his wife in his arms. They held each other and cried because that was all they could do.

When Austin replayed the scene in his dreams, he shot the Trooper-In-Charge and freed the children. He usually awoke feeling good about himself, smiling and stretching, until he remembered the truth. The festering, stinking truth. The truth always left a rotten taste in his mouth and put a frown on his face. He hated the truth because it made him hate himself.

Months later, he came home from work after a rough shift and was looking forward to hugging his wife and looking in on his sleeping daughter. He opened the door cheerfully, but his "Honey I'm home!" was met with silence. He stood at the door for a minute, then went through the house, looking for his family. They weren't there, but their stuff was. No signs of quickly packed suitcases, and a call to his wife went straight to voicemail. More calls placed to friends of the family also failed to provide any information. Was no one answering their phones today?

Austin was in a panic. What had happened to them? He looked all over the house for clues. When he couldn't find anything, he sat staring at the wall for about an hour, thinking intently. Nothing. He went into work to see if he could figure out anything at the police station.

His co-workers weren't surprised to see him. Austin was a chronic over-worker and seeing him at the office on his off days and not clocked in was nothing new. Austin sat down at his desk, poured himself some leftover coffee and went to work.

Austin spent a couple of hours combing through police reports for incidents that might have included his family to no avail. Then he ran his wife and daughter's social security numbers in every database he could think of. Nothing. It was like they had just disappeared. After 15 years of marriage, could his wife just run off, and taken his daughter with her? Could that be what it was? He mulled that idea over for a bit, then discounted it. They were at least mostly happily married, and his wife Amy wasn't the type of woman to just let something go. If she had been angry at Austin, she would have given him a piece of her mind, not just slink off without saying anything or at least without leaving a note to get the last laugh.

Then, he had an awful feeling. He thought of his SWAT mission with the Special Services, and a cold sweat ran down his back. He knew something awful had happened to them, he just didn't know what, but somehow – he knew. He felt like he was going to be sick. He stood over a trashcan for a couple of minutes and started to dry heave. Nothing came up but a little bit of bile, and he wiped his mouth with relief that it wasn't puke.

When he was done feeling sorry for himself, he went over to the designated Special Services database at work. He had never used this computer before and he had to ask for help with how to use it. After one of the other officers came over to help him turn it on and showed him how to use the machine, he got it working and looked his wife and daughter up. What he found made him feel sick to his stomach again. He thought he might vomit this time. Then the urge passed and he was able to continue reading.

As it turns out, the Special Services had conducted "anti-terrorist" operations at his daughter's grade school last night. After reading the Special Services Department after-action report, it was unclear if the grade school was the intended target or not or had just been collateral damage. Austin had a bad feeling and suspected the worst. He called in some favors and his friend helped him figure out which morgue the bodies from the raid had been brought to. When he had an address, he raced down there.

Austin flashed his badge at the morgue and was led into a small, white, clean room with dozens of bodies lying on gurneys. The doctor went with him and helped him view the bodies. After a few charred bodies he found his wife. She was almost burned beyond recognition, but they were able to identify her through dental records. He stared at her body through his tears. His daughter Melisa's body was less mangled, but still badly burnt. He tried to make it to the bathroom so he could vomit into a toilet. He wasn't successful, and instead, stood retching his guts out in the hallway outside the exam room.

He learned later that the Special Services had gotten a tip that HLF fighters were meeting at his daughter's school and had gone to raid it without doing any research. If they had checked into the tip, they would have found out that the gathering at the school was a Christmas play, and the tip that they were acting on had been called in as a prank by a 10-year-old who was grumpy that she hadn't gotten the play's leading role. Austin's daughter Melisa was in the play's chorus and had been very proud of her background role as a Christmas Octopus. His wife had gone to film the play for her husband and had been sitting in the audience with the other parents and family members. Austin couldn't believe he had completely forgotten that the play was tonight and cursed his over-dedication to a job that had made him miss so much of their lives.

The Troopers had burst through the auditorium's side entrance right in the middle of the play's second act. When a school administrator screamed in shock from the sudden appearance of the armed men, one of Troopers started shooting, and all the other Troopers joined in. Someone threw a grenade, and pieces of kids and parents alike were blown all over the place. When he realized his mistake, the Trooper-In-Charge decided that it would be far easier to kill the survivors than to do the paperwork that was required to issue an official Special Services apology. He directed another Trooper to let loose with a flamethrower and they burned everyone in the auditorium to a crisp like they were at a cookout.

Austin took little comfort in the knowledge that his family members weren't to be eaten. He knew that decision was more due to the use of the military grade flamethrower that made the seared human flesh inedible than out of consideration for his family. He was not consoled to hear that the government would be paying for his family members funerals. He went home to an empty house with an empty heart. He stared at the walls and slowly his heart filled with hate. Hatred for those who had killed his family and hatred for those that had poisoned the country he loved.

Austin stood and once more looked at himself in the bathroom mirror. He could feel Amy and Melisa there with him, and he broke down once again.

Through his tears, he spoke to them. "Amy, I'm going to make them pay for what they've done. I'm going to make them pay in blood for what they did to you and our baby girl."

There was no answer, only silence. He looked again at his reflection, and again he promised his dead wife and his murdered child vengeance. Then he punched the mirror, again and again, and smiled through the tears as glass bit into his skin, smashing his reflection, and sealing his fate with a blood oath.

CHAPTER 6

Later that night at Rob and Maria's house, there was a knock on the door. The night was strangely cold, and rainy. The rain was pouring so hard it was hard to hear anything, let alone the knocking on the door. Rob cautiously answered the door. It was Gloria's friend Melanie, and she was crying so hard it took several minutes before she was able to talk.

"They got her." She sobbed uncontrollably, shaking with fear. "They got Ria."

"Who got her? What happened?" Rob asked.

"Them…the- the- the- men in black. The SS."

Melanie told them what she had witnessed at the protest. The family was in a panic, stricken with grief and worry. Maria broke down crying. Rob, seeing his wife in that state, told her that they would go to the police and get back their daughter. Rob and John jumped into the family car and drove to the police station. After a long drive through winding, pothole-filled streets, and a couple of close calls with drunk drivers, they finally made it there.

They took a number and waited in line for five hours before they were able to talk to an officer. The waiting was pure torture. When it was finally their turn, they pleaded their case. They showed the officer Gloria's picture, along with John's veteran card, which guaranteed them exemption from "Project Carnivore."

The officer's name was Joseph Campbell. He was a twenty-year veteran of the police force. He was a fat, angry man, and was frumpily dressed, as that was all his salary would afford him. While the SS lived well on their high salaries, the local police forces did not.

Officer Campbell stared at the girl's picture for a while, and then at the veteran card. He sighed. Then he spoke:

"Look, I'm going to level with you, there probably isn't that much that I can do. I can make some calls, but I can't guarantee anything. Even if I was able to find out where she was, I probably wouldn't be able to get her freed. At this point if she was picked up as a "terrorist" (he made the air quotes when he said terrorist for emphasis), her exemption due to her connection to your veteran status wouldn't apply. Also, it will be costly."

"How much?" John asked.

"Five thousand dollars to make some calls. Up front. I can only guarantee the attempt, not the result."

Campbell saw their frowns and responded, "Look guys, justice ain't cheap you know. It's up to you. Take it or leave it. There is a cash machine down the hall. If you choose to go this route, come back with the money within 3 hours and ask for me directly. Don't take a number or you will be back in that fucking miserable line again."

They stood in the hallway and debated the merits of a system that forced them to bribe the police to do their jobs. It was a short conversation as they both knew that this was the only way forward. After about five minutes they walked down the hall to find the cash machine.

There was a long line at the cash machine as well. They were bored standing in line, so Rob started up a conversation with the guy in front of them. It turned out he was also getting money to barter for the release of a child, as was the guy behind them.

After about 2 hours they finally got the money and headed back to the find Officer Campbell. When they got back to his office, they asked for him, but they were told that he was in the bathroom and that they would have to wait.

Thirty minutes later, Campbell returned from the bathroom, sweating. He looked at both and sighed. Then he took the money, the photo of Gloria and her personal information and told them to wait outside the office and he would call them when he found out what was going on.

Rob and John sat on the bench outside the office. They were anxious to know the truth but scared of what they might be told. They could only come up with so much small talk to fill the space, talk of better days, and less crazy times. After several hours they were called back into Campbell's office. They were both exhausted.

"Ok, I have some good news and some bad news. The good news is that she is alive. I can even tell you which facility that they are keeping her in, and it might be possible to arrange a "payment" to get her back."

Campbell wiped his sweaty brow and continued.

"Well, there is no easy way to say this. The bad news is that they are going to want $500,000 to get her back. Also, since she is at the Dairy Farm, they are probably ugh…raping her as we speak. The $500,000 will help to get her back, but there are no guarantees to what condition she will be in. Raped, beaten, missing an arm, an eye, maybe even dead. And sometimes the Dairy Farm refuses the money."

Campbell was genuinely sorry for their misfortune. No matter how many times he had to tell families bad news it never got any easier.

John and his dad didn't know how to react at first. John punched the wall until his hand bled, while Rob steadied himself because he felt like he might pass out. After they collected themselves, Rob spoke.

"What should we do if we want to go ahead with this?" asked Rob.

"Well, you have two options. Option number 1 is to have me broker the exchange. For that I would need $10,000 non-refundable, in cash, up front- plus the $500,000, also in cash. We go together to the Dairy Farm and attempt to buy back your little girl. This is your best bet to get your daughter back, and to do it safely.

"Option number 2 is that you go it alone, but I can't guarantee your safety if you do this, or that you'll even get to see your daughter. Remember, the usual rate to buy someone back is $1,000,000, but I got you a VETERAN'S discount. There it is. What will it be?"

John and his dad looked at each other. Obviously the $500,000 – oh yeah, $510,000 -was going to ruin the family. They would have to re-mortgage the family home at 50% APR, and with these tough times they would most certainly end up homeless. Still, Gloria was family, and how do you put a price on the life of a family member?

"Ok, we'll pay," said Rob. "What next?"

"Alright. How long will it take for you to come up with the money?"

"I can have the money by tomorrow at 3 PM," declared Rob.

"It is already 5 in the morning, so do you mean 3 PM as in 10 hours from now or tomorrow as in the next day?

Rob looked at his son, and back at Campbell. "Sorry, I mean in 10 hours, at 3 PM today.

"Good, see you in 10 hours here with the money. With any luck we'll get your daughter back alive. Try not to worry, and at least take a nap, you look like a mess."

Rob was shitting himself with worry the whole drive back home. He knew that resistance against the government was futile. They drove past the execution of some political prisoners on the street. The Troopers were making a big show of it, and even had a live band playing while they killed the prisoners to the beat of the music.

When they got back Rob didn't even have to say anything, Maria just knew. She started to sob.

"They have our baby girl, but I have a plan to get her back," Rob said.

Maria couldn't speak, she just continued to cry.

Rob filled her in on the details. This was going to ruin them financially, but what alternative did they have? Let their daughter die? There was only one option: pay the money. Life would never be the same again. Rob didn't know how to handle the stress and he also cried himself to sleep.

CHAPTER 7

At long last daybreak came. Rob and Maria didn't sleep at all. They were able to get the additional mortgage on their home with a phone call, and after a trip to the bank they sat there staring at the open briefcase of money on the kitchen table. They hardly spoke, knowing the awful truth: things would never be the same again.

John woke up exhausted. He hadn't slept well either. He was anxious for his parents and for his sister. He went downstairs and greeted his parents. They were obviously dead tired and looked wrought with worry. The pain in their eyes made his heart ache and he wanted to cry as well. The suffering of his parents was truly awful, and he prayed for a quick resolution to this wide-awake nightmare.

Their breakfast had no taste to it. It wasn't a real breakfast anyway, as it was already past noon. They ate cereal and drank coffee in silence and pondered what the day had in store for them. John resolved to be strong for his father and mother. He had been fucked up for years after the Army and they had stuck by him, thick and thin no matter what. The least he could do is be by their side. Hopefully they would all be able to get through it together.

The time came to go to the police station. Maria protested, but Rob was adamant that she stayed at home while he and John went and made the exchange. He was sure the horrors of the Dairy Farm were going to be too much for her to handle. He had no idea how he himself was going to get through all of this. He thought he might lose it at any point and break down crying. John, on the other hand, seemed to be doing ok. Rob looked at his son. John had an icy resolve, that once activated, meant that he could accomplish anything. He had the same look in his eye as the day that he left for the Army, Airborne School, Ranger School, and for his first deployment.

They arrived at the police department five minutes early and went to Campbell's office. Campbell was there ready to great them.

"Did you guys get any sleep? Nah I guess I wouldn't be able to sleep either. The money- my cut first, then the $500,000?"

Campbell counted his ten grand and put it in a safe. Next, he took the briefcase from Rob and cuffed it to his hand.

"Let's not take any chances. I hate dealing with the Dairy Industry. They are fucking crooked and will stab you in the back and then rape your corpse."

Rob and John looked at each other. They didn't say a word. Officer Campbell motioned for them to follow him. They went out of the back of the police station and got into his Bronze Patrol Car. Rob and John sat in the back like criminals, and they felt helpless in this situation. They needed this man to help them get Gloria back, but could they trust him? Well, they would find that out soon enough. They drove to the outskirts of town, where it was rural and near other farms.

They knew they were getting closer by the smell. While neither Rob nor John had been to a Dairy Farm before, they had heard rumors of its bad smell. The stench was a vile collection of shit, piss, and other bodily fluids. There was no toilet provided for the human "cows" and they were expected to relieve themselves where they slept. John imagined that it was part of the process to de-humanize them. It's sick what humans will do to other humans, he thought.

The Dairy Farm had an industrial look to it. The complex had high gates and fences and still bore the billboards of a previous generation of "happy" cows who seemed content to be raped and abused for their whole lives. What irony, John thought. The oppressive system that had once murdered cows for profit was simply refitted to do the same to humans, and then it was back to business as usual, just with a different species of animal to abuse.

Officer Campbell parked the patrol car in the spot marked "official business only" and turned off the engine. After a deep sigh, looked at the two of them.

"Just keep your mouths shut and let me do the talking and everything will probably be alright. This place is disturbing but keep your fucking comments to yourself. Are we clear?"

They both nodded in agreement. Without saying a word, all three of them exited the car. The air was foul even outside, and though it was cold and raining, none of them were excited to enter. They stood outside the gate, pausing for a moment to gather their collective strength, before Campbell pushed the intercom bell. After a few minutes a deep male voice finally answered.

"Yes.'

"This is Officer Campbell. I am here about that business that we had discussed earlier."

After a long pause, the voice finally spoke again.

"Ok, I have to discuss this with my supervisor."

They waited for a couple of minutes, but the suspense was nerve- racking. They stood there in the rain, teeth chattering, waiting. John looked up and watched the raindrops fall down on him until his face was wet. Rob was so worried he thought he might vomit. His little girl was in this awful place. What would he tell his wife if he wasn't able to get her back?

Finally, the intercom squawked to life once again. "Ok. Your visit is confirmed. You may enter the facility."

The thick metal door slowly screeched open, and the three of them walked inside. It was warm inside the farm, and they were momentarily relieved to be out of the rain. That thought was fleeting, because it was quickly replaced with one of dread and despair. The bleak interior of the Dairy Farm was one of an endless number of stalls filled with women. They were chained to the floor, and all were without clothes. The women's only identifying marks were their tattoo brands that declared them as property of the farm. The air hung heavy with the collective sounds of crying, shrieks of pain, and the whirl of industrial farming equipment.

An armed guard came over to greet them. He wore a grey jumpsuit with the facility name embroidered on it, and a helmet and visor that made it hard to see the man's face. As the guard turned his head John noticed that the guy was wearing ear plugs, presumably to block out the noise. He also noted that the guard carried a beanbag shotgun and a stun baton. John mused that while being hit with either of those weapons would hurt, they weren't lethal weapons. The guard introduced himself as Lewis and told them that he would bring them to the boss.

Lewis led them down the countless aisles of stalls. John noticed that there were women of all ages and races imprisoned here. Some of the women were hooked to machines, which Lewis explained was to do the milking. A contraption that looked like a demonic version of a steampunk bra was attached to each woman's breasts. The devices gyrated and whined, producing a white liquid that was pumped through tubes to a gigantic central breast milk bladder in the middle of the facility. John watched the liquid as it traveled from the various women's breasts through the tubes and remarked that it looked like some of the breast milk had blood in it.

Lewis laughed at the expression on John's face. "Oh yeah, there is actually A LOT OF BLOOD in the breast milk. Don't worry, we dye the final product white, so it all looks like milk."

Some of the women were being raped in their stalls and their screams bit through the air. The whimpering cries of one of the girls got John's attention. He stopped at her stall and watched in horror as two men took turns violating her as they gave each other drunken high fives. The girl was young – probably around John's sister's age –and her naked body was covered in blood and feces. The girl had a look of sadness and utter despair, and her eyes met John's for a moment, as if to say "help." John stepped forward to intervene but was stopped by Lewis before he could

do anything.

"Look," said Lewis. "This isn't rape. This is just business.

This human cow is property of the Dairy Farm, and for a nominal

fee, anyone can participate in the insemination process. To

interfere with the process is a felony offense and violators will be

prosecuted under the Human Agriculture Act of 2045. Also, we'll

kick your ass out of the facility, and you can forget ever seeing

your sister again."

John hesitated. He knew right from wrong, and this was

clearly wrong. However, he didn't want to do something that

would jeopardize getting his sister back. He dropped his head and

backed up. The guard smiled, and they moved on. Rob tried to

change the topic.

"What happens to the babies?" asked Rob.

"Oh, they become veal. Very tender and delicious,

especially if paired with the right wine."

John and his dad shot each other a grimace. Rob thought

he might be sick this time and told himself to keep it together.

The desire to get out of here and flee this place was almost uncontrollable, but they knew that they had to get Gloria back and rescue her from this hell, no matter what it took.

After some time, they walked clear to the other side of the factory and came to a set of steps. The guard led the way up the steps to the second-floor office. An SS Trooper stood outside the door and told them to wait while he received permission for them to enter. When he got the word, he buzzed them into the office.

The Trooper led them into the office. John and Rob were astounded by what they saw. The office was decorated like a medieval throne room. An actual throne sat in the back of the room, and the walls were adorned with gold. A naked woman with a collar around her neck played the harp. John's sister Gloria sat naked on all fours on the ground next to the throne, like a dog might have. A man dressed in a black SS uniform sat upon the throne, guarded by three SS Troopers. He had a smile on his face and a riding crop in his hand. He lightly tapped the palm of his other hand with the crop while he stared at them, almost through them. Then, he spoke.

"Welcome to the farm. I know that my decorating tastes might be a little - how shall I put it-ostentatious?"

The man shot them a big, toothy smile as John and Rob came to grips with what they were seeing. After a brief pause, the man continued.

"But this makes it more comfortable for me, and what is the point of life if you aren't to be comfortable? Relax, make yourselves at home. My name is Riker. How can I help you?"

Riker was 6'5", with a bodybuilder's physique and short blonde hair. He extended his hand, and despite their misgivings all three men shook it. The sound of cracking knuckles and the grunts of pain were music to his ears. Riker smiled broadly; he loved doing this to people. If there was a grade for sadism, Riker would have received an A++.

John, Rob, and Officer Campbell shifted uneasily and looked around the room. Seeing Gloria naked in this place made John and his dad very uncomfortable. It would obviously be impossible for them to relax here. After a moment Campbell broke the awkward silence.

"We've come to make the trade that we spoke of. The $500,000 that we agreed upon, over the phone, in exchange for the girl. It's all here in this briefcase. Just like we discussed."

Riker arose from his throne and walked around the room, swatting things- and people- with his riding crop. After circling the room, he came back to Gloria, and patted her on the head. He returned his attention to them once more and frowned.

"How does one come up with a price for a human life? All that they are, all that they ever will be? How does one determine that? It really is a funny thing, isn't it? To contemplate the value of life. What an interesting topic of conversation."

Riker sighed. "Unfortunately, she is no longer for sale. I appreciate you coming out all this way, in this rotten weather, but I can't sell her to you."

"What? We had a deal. We just talked on the phone a couple of hours ago. We came all the way out here, and I brought the girl's family out here," Campbell said, visibly flustered.

"You are correct. We HAD a deal. Past tense. After that call, I had her brought up here to see what all the fuss was about, and I had to sample her for myself, and let me tell you. She is worth WAY more than $500,000! After fucking your daughter, sir, I've decided that I want to continue to fuck your daughter every day until I grow tired of her. At which point, maybe, I'll cut her up into pieces and eat her, just to sample her soul. "

Rob lunged out to grab Riker by the throat, but Riker was too fast, and easily side- stepped him. John tried to reel his dad in, but it was too late. The Troopers began to beat Rob, and when he fell to the ground, they kicked him as well. John's father grunted with each blow and John moved to help his dad but one of the guards stepped in and stuck a gun in his face. There were five armed guards in this room, and there were only two of them, and they were unarmed. It was unclear at this time if Campbell would be neutral or if he would jump in on their side, but either way they were outnumbered and outgunned.

Riker chuckled. "Oh, this really is too much fun! How can I ever thank you for coming to visit me? Should I send your father back with you alive, or should we send him to the slaughterhouse too?"

John slowed his breathing and calmed himself down. He wanted revenge, but he was in no position to make anything happen now. He would need a gun and a couple of other likeminded soldiers to make things right. He promised himself that he would come back and make this smug son of a bitch regret his decision to fuck with his family. In the meantime, though, pretending defeat was the better move.

"Please sir, stop beating my father. We came all this way in good faith, and we just want to get Gloria back home."

Riker shook his head. "Ok, I guess you are just disappointed. Fair enough. Listen, I'll tell you what. I am a reasonable man, so I am going to make you a NEW deal. Give me the $500,000 and I'll let the two of you walk out of here alive. Otherwise, I can guarantee you that tonight I make a hamburger out of you and your dad and feed it to your sister."

John agreed, and Campbell handed the money over. John helped Rob get to his feet and almost carried his father out of the building. The walk back to the car was strange, as both John and his dad kept their anger to themselves. Campbell didn't know what to say.

When they finally got back to the car, Campbell was the first to speak. "That's the first time something like that has ever happened. I'm really sorry that it ended up sour."

They drove the rest of the way back in silence. Rob was choking back the tears. He had no idea how he was going to tell his wife what had happened. He felt like he was stuck in a nightmare that he couldn't wake up from. He felt helpless, worthless, and scared for his daughter. He wished it had been him that had been taken instead of her.

John, on the other hand, had already started to plot how he was going to get his sister back from those assholes.

CHAPTER 8

For the first time in years, John slept like a baby. The nightmares were finally over. His feelings of guilt and self-doubt were replaced with a profound sense of purpose and clarity. He had been searching for a reason to live, and now he finally had one: to get his sister back or die trying. It really was that simple; everything else was just details.

John thought back to his years in the Army and all the awful shit he had to do to people. He killed the enemy pretty much any way he had to: shoot 'em, stab 'em, bash their brains in with a rock if he had to. Once he set a roomful of guerillas on fire and watched them burn to a crisp. Their screams of terror had filled the night. Now he was going to bring the hurt to these SS motherfuckers, and they were going to wish they had just given him his sister back. Hell, he was going to make them wish they had never been born. The thought of setting SS Troopers on fire made John glow with happiness.

John woke up, had breakfast, and went for a walk to clear his head and to think. Even though it was cold and rainy, the hate basked him in warmth like a lovely summer day. He walked down the street, humming a tune, a golden oldie by a band called Slayer.

He turned the corner and it was as if life just fell into place for him. An SS Trooper had a bunch of teenagers with their hands up against the wall. The Trooper had already beaten one of the kids half to death and he was threatening to shoot the kids if they didn't tell him what he wanted to know.

"I swear to fucking god, I will blow your heads CLEAN OFF, one by one, if you don't give me a name! Who is your contact in the…?"

Before the Trooper was able to finish his sentence, John walked up behind him and punched him as hard as he could in the back of the head. The SS Trooper immediately crumbled like a tin can. John stood over the Trooper for a moment, as if to admire his handiwork. He then picked the Trooper's SD Megablaster pistol (or blaster pistol for short) off the ground. After checking to make sure there was a bullet in the chamber John switched the safety off and aimed the massive pistol at the unconscious Trooper's head. John's finger fidgeted with the trigger, and he intentionally slowed his breathing as he anticipated the kill.

One of the kids stopped him, grabbing his arm –

"No! The shot will bring every fucking Trooper in the whole city down on us!" We got to go! Come with us. My cousin Rudy will know what to do!"

John took the pistol and jammed it into his belt. He grabbed three extra mag reloads from the Trooper's belt, feeling safer already. He kicked the Trooper in the face for good measure and turned and ran.

John followed the kids down back alleys and winding streets. They ducked and weaved through corridors and wound up in a dingy basement. John looked around. Teenagers were hanging out, engaged in the usual activities that teens did to pass the time- get high or fuck. A teenager with short hair and a black eye spoke.

"You helped my cousin back there.

"Yeah. You must be Cousin Rudy."

"That's me. Why did you help my cousin and the other kids back there?"

"Those SS motherfuckers have my sister. We tried to bribe them, but they just took the money, beat my dad almost to death and told us to get fucked. Payback is a motherfucker, and I took it out on the first motherfucker I came across, who just happened to be threatening those kids. Now that I have a gun, I'm going to free my sister from the Dairy Farm or die trying."

Rudy stared at him. "You realize this is pretty much hopeless and that there isn't much if anything you can do, right? That it's all pointless?"

John laughed. "Yep. You think I don't already know that?"

"Then why?"

John shifted. "I was in the Army, and the war fucked me up bad. There were some days I just wanted to die. Then those SS fucks took my sister Gloria, and voila! I have something to live for again. I need to get my sister back or die trying. I at least owe my parents that."

"You said they brought your sister to the Dairy Farm? Well, I know some people who might be able to help. Follow me into the sewers."

CHAPTER 9

John followed Rudy into the very stinking bowels of the city sewers. At first John had been hesitant to enter the manhole, for he was worried about rats. John had always feared rats ever since he was a little boy. Now that he was down in the sewers, stomping around in the dirty water, he remembered that the rats were also dead.

After the virus had mutated back in 2044 it spread from humans to farms and killed off the remaining live -stock animals. People turned to hunting to fill their need for meat, but the virus was resilient and killed off all wild animals. It soon spread to domestic animals, and within 6 months all non- human land animals were dead. No insects, birds, lizards, not even cockroaches were left alive to keep us humans company.

"Nothing down here now except us and the germs," he said out loud, thinking it was weird that he might miss rats. His voice made an eerie echo as it bounced off the walls.

John reached up to his face and felt his mask. He was very glad for its protection in this filthy environment. Rudy made a noise, like a whistle but more animal -like. John watched her, and then looked ahead. There was a light flickering in the distance, and the whistle was returned.

They sloshed on down the corridor, and when they turned the bend, they were surprised to find three masked, hooded figures armed with pistols and machetes. The figure closest to them pointed their pistol at John, telling him to raise his hands and lower his mask. John did as he was told, somewhat amused by the absurdity of it all.

"The fuck you smiling at?! You think I'm cute or something?!" a hostile voice said menacingly in John's direction.

"Yep," John said, still smiling.

Rudy stepped in between them. "Easy Joe. I saw this guy knock out an SS Trooper. He's ex-military or something. He's on the fucking level."

The hooded figure lowered his gun, thought for a moment, then said, "Ok, follow me."

They slipped through a barely perceptible crack in the wall and followed the hooded figures through a narrow crevice. After about 50 meters they came to a small room.

John stepped into the light and looked around.

"This used to be a control room for the old sewers. Now it is long forgotten, but not by us."

The figures took off their masks. Their leader Joe was a man about 25 years old, skinny, with ratty long hair, bad teeth, and a scar under his right eye. The other two were females, in their 20s to 30s, short- haired and worn- out looking. They could almost pass for men in the dark. John wondered if that might have been intentional.

"So, I hear you have an axe to grind with Project Carnivore," Joe said. His voice was squeaky and unsure sounding. He was much tougher looking with a mask on. He looked more like a scared kid than a resistance fighter.

"Yeah, those scumbags took my sister. I'm fixing to get her back, or at least make them sorry for fucking with my family."

"I'm sorry to hear that. I think we can help each other. Our group has been working for years to dismantle the Meat and Dairy industries. A lot of good people have died in the process. Using homemade explosives, we've blown up a car here and there and made things annoying for them, but we haven't made any real progress yet. Now that we have these (pointing to the guns), things are going to be different." Joe took a long look at John, sizing him up. "Rudy says that you have military experience. Were you in the war?"

"That's right," John said.

"Ready to go to war again?" the skinny man asked.

"Shit," said John, with a sigh. "Might as well."

CHAPTER 10

John, Joe, and the rest of the would–be-warriors entered the HLF Headquarters. The fetid air was dank and smelled of old farts, grease, and sewage. Some of the HLF members were standing around a table, gawking at a bunch of crudely built machine guns. An older black man was teaching a class on how to use the guns. He stopped when John and Joe walked in and introduced himself.

"Hi, my name is Austin. I used to be a cop and now I'm the leader of this rag-tag bunch of misfits. I went from being a law enforcement officer to an outlaw in less than 3 months." Austin laughed at his own joke. Obviously, this was a joke he enjoyed telling.

"Well, looks like I'm in the right spot, because I'm a misfit too. I'm John."

"Nice to meet you, John. We are having a class on some of the new additions to our homemade arsenal. Please join us." Austin raised his gun to show John, and the class continued.

"Since the government outlawed guns and no one has

them anymore, they won't be expecting us to be armed. One of our guys found a video on how to make one of these on something called "You Tube" that was left on an outdated server. It's called a Blyskawica and was created by Polish freedom fighters one hundred years ago during World War Two. It is hard to say and even harder to spell correctly, but it is cheap and easy to make just using simple tools. We have a bunch of them."

"It's crude, but it will usually fire and that's the most important thing. It operates from an open bolt, so to fire pull back the charging handle," Austin pulled back the charging handle, and the gun made a ratcheting cocking sound. "And then simply pull the trigger."

"Of course, you would have a loaded magazine in it already before you did that. We did not make a safety, so if you want to make the weapon safe, pull the trigger and ease the charging handle back in place. We also didn't make a selector switch, so when you pull the trigger, this weapon will continue shooting until it jams or runs out of ammo."

"When firing, I suggest you try for controlled, short bursts instead of the mag dump you might see in movies. It will be more accurate than a mag dump. This gun might get away from you if you do a mag dump."

"I wouldn't call this the most accurate gun, or the easiest to shoot, or the most reliable. Sometimes it will shoot and sometimes it will jam. The magazines that we made suck, but it can also fit the standard SS 9mm mags, so use their mags when you can. It shoots a standard 9mm bullet, so there will always be ammo for them. We have about a thousand bullets from reloading bullet shell casings that we've found."

Austin looked around the room. He guessed most of these new volunteers had never even held a gun before, let alone shoot one at another person. He saw more than one of the kids flinch at the sound of the bolt moving forward, and he didn't like that. Jumpiness gets you killed. He noticed that the new guy John seemed comfortable around the guns. Military perhaps?

Austin continued. "Hmm, what else. Oh yeah, we borrowed the wire stock from the grease gun. Simply pull it out to extend it and push it back in to make it more portable."

"Also, note the threaded barrel. That's for a suppressor, or as you would call it, a silencer. To add the suppressor, simply screw it on like this and tighten it. While it won't make the gun completely silent it will be a lot less loud, almost stealthy, though you are probably going to have to hit them a bunch more times to kill them since it weakens the damage caused by the gunshot. "

"Lastly, let me suggest that you should aim center mass with this gun. Aim for the chest, not the head. These bullets are going to go all over the place, and if you aim for the head, you are likely to miss. If you aim for the chest, you are likely to get a few rounds in the chest and a few shots to the chest are all it takes.

"This," He pointed to the shotgun pistol for emphasis, "Is deadly at close range."

"We also have a few of these shotgun pistols. They are not super accurate, but they will decimate whatever gets in front of them at 10 feet or less. After that, they are pretty much worthless."

"They take two 12-gauge slugs. You load them by disengaging this latch to break the gun down, inserting the slugs and then closing the weapon. Once you have fired both shots you have to break the gun down again to reload."

Austin turned to John. "I heard you got a SD

Megablaster pistol."

"Yep." John pulled it out and showed everyone, thinking that this was a lot like 'show and tell" at school.

Austin continued. "Have you ever shot one of those before?"

John shook his head. "I've shot other guns before, but nothing like this."

"I used to carry one of those when I was a Bronze," said Austin, shaking his head. "Expect a big kick. The point of those guns is shock and awe. They are impractical and not at all fun to shoot, but they will do some wicked damage. Really big magnum bullet, with an explosive tip. Aim straight for center mass, and it will punch a hole through a person the size of a softball. It will also go through body armor, so save those shots for when you fight someone with a vest."

"The 9mm bullets will bounce off the vest. This blaster will make a mess out of a vest. You can almost shoot through tank armor with that gun. "

Austin picked up a long silver cylinder.

"We also have a few pipe bombs. You'll have to light

them and throw them. The fuses are unreliable at best, but the result will be awesome."

"Oh yeah, and we got these," showing off a crude looking grenade. "These chemical grenades will make people puke, and their eyes tear up. We are going to be wearing gas masks and pop these as we enter. That will give us a momentary advantage as things pop off. We must make sure that we move quickly, so we don't lose the advantage. We have bags made up with ammo, and one of each of the guns here."

"So, here's the plan…"

KA-BOOM!!!!!

An explosion rocked the room and smoke wafted all around them. John felt pain in his ears, immediately knowing that those were flash bang grenades and that this was a raid. "Fuck!" he thought "it can't be over already." Gunshots entered the room, and shrieks of pain came from hit HLF fighters. Austin got to his feet, picked a submachine off the table, and shot at the unseen Troopers through the smoke.

Austin then turned and yelled to those who could hear -

"Grab the guns and go!"

John grabbed two of the shotgun pistols off the table and emptied them both into the first two SS Troopers he saw. The unlucky Troopers disappeared into blood and gore as John literally wiped the determination clean off their faces.

Dropping the shotgun pistols on the ground, John took a submachine gun and a satchel of filled magazines off the table. John rocked the gun's charging handle back and sent a quick burst into the next guy, taking him off his feet and leaving him in a mangled pile. John quickly noted that none of the SS were wearing body armor, and his confidence grew.

Holding the submachine gun like a pistol, John sprayed the rest of the magazine into the next group of Troopers and turned and ran after the survivors. On the way out he grabbed one of the gear bags and dropped two live grenades behind him to cover their tracks.

CHAPTER 11

John, Austin, Joe, and the rest of the survivors fled through the sewer labyrinth for 2 hours till they finally stopped to catch their breath. Austin turned his gaze towards Joe.

"How did they find us?" he asked in a quiet voice.

Joe shrugged.

John sensed a weird tension between them and wondered what was going on. Time seemed to slow down as they stood staring at each other in the middle of the sewer corridor. It almost looked like they were squaring off like in a Western movie showdown. The younger man suddenly went for the gun in his belt. The older man was quicker on the draw and stuck what looked like an old-fashioned 1911 government automatic right in the squeaky man's face.

"Talk."

Joe started to cry. "They took my family hostage. They said they would kill and eat them if I didn't lead them to our hideout. I had to do it. I had to. I didn't have a choice."

Austin scowled.

"There is always a choice."

Austin shot Joe through the temple. The squeaky man dropped like a rock, splashing to the sewer floor. Austin looked around at the group, then shot Joe again for good measure.

John didn't know what he had expected the Human Liberation Front to be like, but this wasn't it. Standing here in the sewers it dawned on John that the government had been lying about the HLF. Obviously, they had overinflated the HLF's capabilities to justify the erosion of citizen's rights and the rounding up of political dissidents. These weren't hardened criminals. These weren't terrorists. They were just scared kids, and this was amateur hour. Some of the younger members started to cry.

Austin counted heads and surveyed the group. There were 10 of them left, which means 15 of them were killed or captured. Austin cleared his throat to get their attention.

"There are a couple ways we could play this," said Austin. "We could go on the defensive and hide, which is what they would expect us to do. We could split up and run, which would make us harder to track, but weaker as a force."

"Or…" he continued. "We could do something unexpected…like attack them! Remember, the best defense is a good offense."

John and the rest of them stirred. They hadn't been expecting that as one of the options. It was a crazy idea, and one of them said so.

"I know what y'all are thinking," said Austin. "It's a crazy idea, but I think that they would be expecting all of the other possibilities. If we attacked somewhere like the Dairy Farm and were able to free the women there, maybe some of them would join us."

Austin had John relay what he saw on his trip to the Dairy Farm. After listening to John's story, Austin considered what John said, and concluded the Dairy Farm was a relatively soft target. Security was lax with not many guards, and they had visitors in there all the time. Perhaps one of them could enter the Dairy Farm under the pretense of paying for sex with one of the human cows, and then open the door for the group. Granted, they didn't have training as a unit, but crazier things have been done.

After hours of trudging through the sewers they finally emerged from underground. They walked the final five miles under the cover of darkness. The group arrived at their destination wet and miserable. Austin led them to a safe house to outfit, plan, and recuperate for the mission. Austin went down the list of people and supplies. Between the 10 of them that were left, there were 7 submachine guns, 4 shotgun pistols, and John's blaster pistol. Luckily there were other guns stashed in the safe house, and a variety of silencers. Austin went to work fitting silencers onto the submachine guns. He found four 9mm pistols in the safe house stash that could be used with silencers. The rest of the group slept, for they were all exhausted.

In the morning John awoke to the hustle and bustle of the team moving throughout the safe house. The house was located far out of town in the middle of nowhere. The building was abandoned long ago and left for dead. Now re-purposed as a headquarters for the Human Liberation Front, it seemed to once again be alive with people moving throughout its halls and walking up and down its stairs. The sounds of squeaking stairs, creaking floorboards, and human chatter echoed through the old house. The smell of coffee brewing on a cook stove wafted all around.

John had slept on the cold, dirty floor, and while he missed his bed, he was happy to be with the team. He had found a military poncho liner blanket, affectionately called a "Woobie" by soldiers and marines and curled up with it on the hard floor. It reminded him of his time in the Army and of his deployments, and of war. Not all bad memories, but a lot of bad in there too.

John was happy to be back on a mission, back in the shit, as he had called it when he was in the Army. He thought that it was ironic that he had tried so hard to forget all about being in the military, but now his survival and possibly the success of the missions might depend on how much he was able to remember.

After hot coffee and a basic meal of rice and canned vegetable stew they got down to business. Austin told them that while everyone was sleeping, information came in from their spy network. They had been able to find out the exact number of guards, inmates, and weapons used at the Dairy Farm. The information was hard to come by and should be considered as valuable as gold.

The spy had told him that the entire Dairy Farm of 100 inmates only had seven security guards and three SS Troopers. Because all the inmates were chained women, security at the Dairy Farm was lax. Most of the security guards didn't carry lethal weapons, only electric batons, and bean bag shotguns. The regular guards were not well trained and were often prisoners themselves. They wouldn't have much fight in them and would go down rather quickly. The SS Troopers, on the other hand, were expected to be armed with at least blaster pistols, maybe even battle rifles. The SS Troopers were highly trained fanatics, and the team should expect them to fight to the death.

Austin produced a piece of paper with a crudely drawn map of the Dairy Farm on it, and everyone huddled around for a mission briefing. The Dairy Farm was shaped like a huge rectangle, with entrances in the front, sides, and rear. First, they would find and subdue the two guards who were patrolling around the perimeter of the building. They then would approach from the front entrance. One of them would knock on the door under the ruse of wanting to bribe a guard for sex with one of the inmates. When the guard opened the door, they would quickly subdue the guard and enter the building.

The guards patrolled around the interior randomly, and it was hard to know exactly where in the building they were at any minute, so they would rely on speed and violence of action to quickly take out the guards and move on to the real threat – the Troopers. Besides having the ability to call into their headquarters for reinforcements, which would put a quick end to the mission, the Troopers were armed to the teeth and spoiling for a fight. They would have to try to catch them off guard to easily subdue them.

Austin looked around the room, making sure that everyone was following the plan. When everyone nodded in agreement, he continued. "Finally, there is a big office on the second floor. We have no idea what or who is in there."

John raised his hand. "It's the lair of an SS asshole named Riker. He has that upstairs office decked out like a throne room. He fancies himself like a king or some stupid bullshit like that. He's holding women hostage in his lair. Last time I was there he had my sister."

Everyone turned and looked at John.

Austin thought it over and then said, "This Riker fellow won't go down easily, and we should expect there to be something that we are missing. People like this often have tricks up their sleeves, so let's plan accordingly. We have tear gas, and explosives that we can use to take the hinges off the doors if we can't force our way through. If we hit them hard and fast, we should be able to overtake them before they have a chance to know what hit them. Then, we free the prisoners, rig the building with explosives, and blow this factory of death sky high."

John noticed one of the HLF fighters staring at him. "What's up?" he asked.

The HLF fighter was named Joy. She was skinny but muscular, with long, black hair she wore in a ponytail that seemed to have a life of its own when she moved. John reckoned she was cute in a tough sort of way.

Joy threw up her arms. "How do we know that this guy isn't going to choke once the bullets start flying?"

John laughed. "You don't. I guess you are going to have to find out the hard way."

"Oh, fucking perfect," Joy retorted in a huff.

John smiled. She was cute even when she was scowling.

They gathered their gear. All 10 members of the team had suppressed submachine guns with 4 magazines of ammo each, plus bolt cutters to free the women, explosives, tear gas, knives, and individual weapons. John had found a Trooper combat vest in the pile of gear that was stuffed in the closets. He was able to put it together with pouches for all his magazines and position them in front on his chest for easy access. It reminded him of the one he had in the Army, except this one was all black. Would it stop a bullet? John decided he didn't want to find out.

Besides his submachine gun, he was also given a captured SS pistol, a COBRA 656. The COBRA 656 was a 9mm pistol that featured a built-in silencer. He decided he would use that pistol to take out the first couple of guards. He didn't completely trust the home-made submachine guns, and those first couple of shots might be the most important ones of the whole mission. His life, and the success of the mission, would rest on them, so he didn't want to risk it all with a makeshift gun if he didn't have to.

He found a double shoulder holster in the pile of gear that was compatible with both his blaster pistol, and the 9mm pistol. John adjusted the holster to his size and put it on. When it fit comfortably, John put a loaded pistol into each side of the holster and snapped them into place.

In the final hours before the mission, John disassembled and cleaned all his weapons. It was a ritual he had learned in the Army. It helped calm his nerves and ensured that the guns would function properly. He meditated to help relax and contemplated his mortality. When he was done, he took a nap. He knew that no matter what the outcome, it was going to be a long night.

CHAPTER 12

The Commander sat in his office with his boots up on his desk, relaxing and thinking about his life. He had been an accountant named Randolph Nibblesworth when all of the chaos of the early 2040's had begun. Then the President abolished Congress, the Supreme Court, and the Constitution, and declared himself "President for Life." A new era for a new America had begun, and with it, the glory of the SS. The Commander felt very lucky to be born at just the right place and at the right time. When else in history would he of had the chance to have so much fun? Also, he liked being called "Commander" much more than the name his parents gave him.

Today had been a busy day, and now he was all tuckered out. He had beaten a child to death and shot another just to make a point about brutality and control. The lesson had been an important one, and he believed in leading from the front. Still, it had taken a lot out of him. His hands still hurt from punching the child in the skull. He had considered putting gloves on, but he thought that would have somehow diminished the statement that he was making about the psychological importance of violence on controlling the population.

The Commander had been out with his men patrolling. He had a limited number of men with him, and the point of the exercise was more to remind the people that the government was watching them than to enforce any laws. He hadn't expected to kill anyone on this patrol, nor did he expect any resistance. The men were lightly armed, only carrying half of their normal combat load, and most of them were not wearing their usual heavy bullet-proof armor.

The patrol was going as planned. They had walked through the town with no issues. Most people had greeted them, and those that didn't looked the other way or tried to pretend that they didn't see them. Yes, there were a few frowns, but nothing other than that. Then a kid gave one of his men the finger.

The boy was there with his family, out in the busy shopping center of town. He was dressed in outlawed fashion style, called "punk rock" – a smiling skull bootlegged t- shirt, camouflage shorts, and skate shoes. He was listening to music and had headphones on, lost in his own world. The child was apparently so lost in his music that he accidentally walked right into one of the Troopers.

"Watch where you're going," the Trooper snarled. It would have been all over then, except the kid told the Trooper to "Fuck off," and gave him the finger. The Trooper didn't seem to know how to react. He hesitated. All eyes were on them. The entire town seemed to stop what it was doing to watch this confrontation.

The Commander slowly walked over to the boy, smiling. The boy took off his headset and addressed him.

"Oh yeah, what are you going to do, Grandpa?"

"Teach you some manners, little boy."

"Oh yeah, you and what Army?"

The Commander's first punch knocked the smirk right off the boy's face. The boy held his broken nose in both hands, blood gushing everywhere and making quite a spectacle. He stared at the Commander. Obviously, the boy had grown up privileged, and mistakenly thought the rules that governed everyone else didn't apply to him. A look of shock and pain had replaced the smile. The Commander was still smiling though, and he commenced to beating the boy mercilessly.

While it would have been a lot easier to have just shot the boy, the Commander thought beating the child to death would be a better way of sending the proper message. Shooting someone and killing them is quick. It looks brutal but the act has a quick time stamp, and it is done. One second alive, the next, a corpse. To beat someone to death, however, takes time. It takes stamina. It takes resolve. It takes a hard heart to beat someone to death, to hit them so many times that they die.

After what seemed like an eternity, the Commander stood up and examined his handiwork. The boy lay in a bloody, mangled, mess. The Commander had caved in the kid's face. The eyes had looked at him, had pleaded with him, so he had gouged them out. The boy's arms had tried to get in the way of the beating, so he had broken them, too. Finally, he grew bored of the violence, so he choked the life out of the boy. All the while people just looked on.

The child had begged. First for his mother, then just cries to stop. The Commander had been a little unnerved by the pleading, and the crying, especially once the child had started to choke on his own blood. The child had just laid there making gurgling noises, until the Commander put his hands around the child's throat and squeezed.

People crowded around to take in the sights and to catch a glimpse of the blood, much in the way that people slow down to look at a car accident. Only the older sister tried to intervene. The parents had stood motionless, understanding what this was, and how quickly they too would meet the same fate if they lifted a finger to help. Their teenage daughter wasn't as lucky. She screamed and hollered and struck a Trooper, calling him a "foul motherfucker" and tried to grab the Commander's hand to stop him from beating her brother.

After the Commander had finished with correcting the boy's behavior, he was now ready for the girl. This girl had tried to stop them from punishing the boy, had struck a Trooper, and had used bad language to address them.

"There must be consequences for such actions," the Commander had said, addressing both the girl and the crowd. "For without consequences for such actions there would be anarchy."

The Commander instructed his men to strip the girl naked, and to rape her. One by one they took their turns with her. The Commander had thought at the time that it was fortunate that this had happened. He was able to teach the public a lesson, and give his Troopers some much needed R&R.

It was then that one of the Troopers made a fatal flaw. While one of the Troopers was raping the girl from behind, another stuck his penis in the girl's face, trying to get the girl to suck it, much like one would see in a porno film. At first the girl pretended to play along, allowing the penis to be inserted into her mouth, but when it was fully inserted, she chomped down and BIT IT OFF!

The wounded Trooper backed away from the girl, screaming and clutching at the stump of what was once his penis. Blood spurt all over the place. The other Trooper stopped his raping and stood in disbelief. All the men in the unit moved uncomfortably away from the girl. The crowd looked from the girl to the Trooper, then to the Commander. What was going to happen next?

The girl spit the bleeding Trooper's severed penis back at

him. It lay like a shriveled sausage on the ground, covered with blood and dirt. The girl got to her feet and smiled.

"ALL YOU MOTHERFUCKERS think you are so strong! You are just COWARDS and little men, beating defenseless children and raping little girls! One day someone will come along and put you in your place! You..."

The girl's words were cut short when a smiling Commander stepped forward and shot her in the head from behind. Brains and bits of skull, eyes, and tongue went everywhere. The screaming Trooper got splashed with most of the gunk, and the rest of it went out into the crowd. Everything was silent after that. Order re-established. Mission accomplished.

Now relaxing at his desk, the Commander warmed when he thought of the girl's bravery. First, she had stood up to them when they were beating her little brother, when even her own parents would not. Then, when she was being brutally raped, she was able to fight back against her attackers and even scar one of them for life. He admired this girl, for she truly had a warrior's spirit. If only his men had her courage, they could squash this rebellion in a matter of days.

CHAPTER 13

John, Austin, and the rest of the group moved through the network of sewers towards the Dairy Farm. As expected, they didn't encounter any resistance along the way, and made fairly good time. Towards the end, however, the walk became a miserable forced march. The sewer stunk, and everyone had sloshy water- logged shoes. John wished that somehow, he had had the insight to wear waterproof shoes for this mission. Wet socks made him miserable.

It was just after midnight when they finally got to the objective. They all huddled up around Austin as he gave the final mission briefing.

"Ok, first we'll take out the outside guards. Then we will assemble around the front entrance. I will approach the door and tell them that I am here for sex...Well, I'm supposed to ask to play a game of pool. There is a whole code that I must go through. When they open the door, we will have to make a game day decision."

"If there is more than one guard at the door, we will

either charge through or I will go in quietly alone. If I go in alone and we don't charge, I'll take care of the guards that I see immediately inside and then open the door. Everyone got the plan?"

The group nodded in agreement. Someone said "okay." John cracked his knuckles, then muttered to no one in particular, "Fuck it, let's do it."

Austin quickly climbed the ladder to the top, paused for a second to give the group a reassuring thumbs up, then removed the manhole cover. Cold rain battered him and everyone else in its path. While an uncomfortable shock to the system after the extreme heat, the chilling rain was a blessing. It was noisy and would help cover the first couple of shots and give them more leeway as they took out the guards. It would also mean that the guards would be less inclined to patrol outside.

Austin waited for a couple of minutes to see if removing the manhole cover had alerted the guards. When he was convinced that it hadn't, he peeked his head out.

Like he had been told, the manhole was only about 30 feet away from the Dairy Farm, and there were a couple of trees nearby that would provide a pretty good place for the group to hide. Austin looked down and waved for everyone else to join him. The rest of the group climbed up the ladder as quietly as they could. After they assembled above ground, Austin led the way over to the trees.

From their cover behind the trees and bushes they stood, watching and waiting in the cold rain for about an hour. During that time only one guard walked by the entrance. Austin surmised that the inclement weather had drastically reduced the roving outside guards. That was good luck for them. Austin handed his submachine gun to a member of the team and pulled out his knife.

"I'll be right back," he said with a grin.

The group watched as Austin noiselessly crept towards the building and then hid in a bush. After about five minutes a guard slowly walked by, head down so as not to get his face wet. Austin pounced on the guard as he walked by, using the man's poor posture to his advantage.

Austin's hand muffled the guard's cries for help as he slit his throat from ear to ear. He then stuck his knife into the base of the guard's skull. The man was dead almost instantly. Austin quietly lowered the body to the ground, went through the man's pockets, and paused. When Austin was sure they hadn't been detected, he gestured for them to move forward. The group did as they were told.

Austin then took off his gear and prepared for his acting debut. He had to look more like a creepy old man looking for sex than a soldier about to do battle. He wasn't sure if he would be able to pull this off and hoped the guards wouldn't question the fact that he hadn't arrived in a car. They all looked at each other. Austin nodded and approached the front door. The rest fanned out and covered Austin with weapons drawn.

Austin pushed the intercom button. Everyone froze, waiting for the exchange that was to come. A voice squawked from the intercom box.

"Who is it? What do you want? Do you know what time it is?"

"Hey. My name is Joe. I heard something about uhh a game of pool?"

"We don't have a pool table."

"Maybe a game of tennis?"

"Who sent you?"

"Melvin the Mop Boy."

Austin was wondering if he had gotten the right information about the Dairy Farm question and password from the spy when the door opened with a loud creak. An obese man with a huge beard and an apron was standing there, barring entry into the Farm.

"You got the money? $500 cash upfront?"

"Oh yes, I have it right here," replied Austin. He fumbled in his pocket, pretending to look for money, then produced a switchblade. The fat man looked down at the knife with surprise. Austin stabbed the man in the chest, pulled it out, and then stabbed him again. The man was so shocked that he didn't yell out or make a sound. Austin stabbed him yet again but still the man didn't fall. John wondered if perhaps it was all the extra layers of blubber that protected the man's vital organs from being punctured.

They all stood there watching the scene unfold and no one moved. Then John stepped forward and drew his silenced

9mm pistol. Standing on his tiptoes, he reached over Austin and put the barrel of his gun directly on the bearded man's forehead and cocked the hammer back. The man looked up just in time to see John shoot him in the face. John placed two shots through the obese man's head in rapid succession. He then looked over and winked at Joy. Joy stuck her tongue out at him.

Austin and John caught the man as he started to fall and then gently pulled his dead body through the doorway so he didn't make a sound inside. The group froze, looking, hearing, and sensing for any detection of their presence. Nothing but the whine of the industrial equipment, the cries and sobs from the women inside, and the stench of unwashed bodies, feces and urine.

They entered the building, splitting up into two teams of five members, each going up one of the two main aisles in a mad dash towards the main office. Austin led the first group and Joy lead the second group, each moving in a single file line with guns drawn.

Instead of thinking of the mission as a life and death struggle, John chose to think of it as a game, a habit he had picked up from his time in the service. This time, the object of the game was speed and stealth. His team was trying to make it to the office with as many of their members alive as possible (without alerting the Farm to their presence). The guards and the other staff were running defense. A touchdown, in this game, would be him literally kicking the severed head of Riker through a goal post. The thought of cutting off Riker's head made John smile.

His daydream almost made him run directly into a guard. The guard stared at John then opened his mouth to yell, but John put a hand over his mouth and shot him twice in the heart. John watched the life flow out of the man's face and then let him fall to the ground. John took up the pace once more, hopping over the guard's twitching body and the pool of blood that lay around it.

John was hyper-aware of the movement of the women and their yelling, crying, and screaming, as well as his own breathing. He was trying to concentrate on possible threats leading up to the office. So far, they had killed two guards and there must be more waiting along the way. He didn't have time to think about how many guards were left or where they might be. They would have to move and shoot like a well-oiled machine, or they would fail. Failure meant death.

Movement towards the right made John slightly turn his head. Just as a guard was raising his shotgun to fire, Joy shot a burst from her silenced submachine gun into him. The guard dropped to the ground like a brick. John gave her a thumbs up and then shot a different guard in the face and chest with his 9mm pistol. John advanced, walking while firing at another guard who stepped into the aisle directly in front of him, placing three shots in a tight group center mass in his chest. John holstered his pistol and transitioned to his submachine, dropping quick bursts into each of the next two guards. A buzzing sound to his back alerted John that another guard had been shot by a teammate. They were getting closer to the objective and John could taste sweet revenge.

John's submachine rocked into action as he took out another guard, then another one. They were now below the office steps and the other half of the unit was approaching. John raised his hand in a thumbs up to Austin, then shot a guard who was lurking in the shadows right behind Austin. Austin breathed a sigh of relief and John changed his magazine. Austin gestured to John that they were headed upstairs. John nodded and pointed to three members of the team to circle up on him.

John, Austin, Joy, and two other HLF members of the team ascended the stairs, while the rest of the team fanned out in a defensive formation below. They climbed the stairs and soon saw what they had been expecting – SS Troopers. What they hadn't been expecting was that the Troopers were asleep! They had been prepared for the worst, and this was the best-case scenario!

Noiselessly, they slunk up the steps towards the guards. They divided into pairs of two, with one in reserve. They held the first Trooper down and stabbed him to death. They then gave the second Trooper a choice: help them open the door or share his fallen comrade's fate. The Trooper didn't need much convincing. He pulled a key from a secret hiding place and they opened the door.

The group burst into the room in commando fashion and was surprised by what they found- no one. No guards, no Riker, no sister. John and Austin looked at each other puzzled.

"Fan out and search the room," whispered Austin. The

team spread out and did as they were told. Joy held the Trooper at gunpoint.

The search produced a couple of battle rifles, a battle sword and a battle knife, bags of money, various handguns and submachine guns, an MG 42 machine gun, computers, uniforms, and a couple of upgraded vests. They put the extra gear and weapons in the center of the room to be distributed among all of them.

John picked out a pair of waterproof duty boots in his size, along with socks, and put them on. He was happy that his feet were no longer wet. Throwing away the wet socks felt like Christmas and his birthday rolled into one. He put on SS combat uniform pants and donned an updated SS combat vest complete with bullet proof panels and magazine pouches. He felt a little heavier, but the weight was well worth it. He grabbed a rucksack to carry some of the extra gear, claiming the battle sword and battle knife for himself. He had a promise to Riker to fulfill, of course.

When they were done with getting all the gear together, Austin questioned the Trooper as to the whereabouts of Riker.

The Trooper replied that he was at his castle. Austin asked him where the castle was and how many guards were there. The Trooper told him how to get to the castle, that it was guarded by 50 Troopers, and that there was no way that they would get in. He added that John's sister was a whore and that they've all taken turns with her. John was taken aback.

"Yes, I remember you. I remember how much fun it was to beat your father right in front of you while you just stood there like a little bitch doing nothing. Yes, we have your sister. She is kept in the throne room at his castle, but you'll never see her again. Not alive at least. Riker is raping her as we speak. HA-HA-HA-HA."

The Trooper continued cackling and talking about how they would never succeed (almost hissing "succeed" like a snake) until John suddenly stabbed him in the chest with the battle knife. The Trooper screamed out in pain and started begging for his life. John pulled the knife out of the Trooper and calmly flipped the "on" switch. The battle knife made a whizzing, whining sound as it came to life. John paused for a second, then hacked the Trooper in the neck.

The battle knife quickly and easily cut through flesh, tendons, and spinal cord. Blood splattered everywhere and one of the girls screamed. The Trooper's body fell to the ground and his head rolled off his shoulders.

Everyone in the room was shocked and there were a few cries and some curses. One person vomited and most of them took a couple of steps back from John, as if there was a fear that the bloodlust was contagious. John just laughed and picked up the head, the eyes still twitching and the mouth still moving. John spat in the face of the decapitated head and soccer kicked it against the wall.

"Motherfuckers would be remiss to think they can treat us this way and then expect civility and kindness in return. I'm done with civility and kindness. All I have to offer them is blood and revenge."

"Fair enough," said Austin. Let's collect everyone and head over to this castle to get your sister."

John was surprised. "Really?"

"Really. We will have an element of surprise if we can get over there quick enough," said Austin.

"We will see if we can get some of the prisoners to fight with us. I'm sure that some of them will. We will send the females who don't want to fight back to another safe house. "

John was a bit skeptical. "Are you sure we shouldn't try to regroup first?"

"Positive. While we regroup, they would have the entire Special Services out looking for us. Our best bet to make this happen would be to attack them again hard before they even know that we hit them here. Strike with all our might. Even if we don't succeed, the attempt will be worth it."

John, Austin, Joy, and the rest of the group went back downstairs with all their new gear. Four HLF fighters were posted to guard the entrances while the rest of them took the keys and went about the task of freeing the women prisoners and removing their masks. John had hoped that maybe what the Trooper had said wasn't true. That maybe, just maybe, his sister had somehow been left behind. As he looked over the 100 or so freed women, he did not see her. She would have to be rescued the hard way.

After all the women had been freed and most of them given some degree of clothing from the SS uniforms, Austin had them all circle around him and then spoke to them.

"Here's the plan. We are going to take some volunteers with us to hit these SS bastards in their castle, especially this big bastard who used to run this place. It's probably going to be very dangerous. These guys are the worst of the worst – not that I need to tell you that – and they aren't going to die easily. Still, we must stick it to them and make it hurt. The rest of you will go with one of our HLF soldiers back to a different safe house. Those that wish to volunteer to go with us, know it is going to be dangerous and step over here."

John could hear the women talking it over.

"Fuck it, let's go kill these assholes," said one.

"I just want to see my family again," said another.

"I'll go, but I don't know if I have it in me to hurt anyone," said another.

Someone said," Fuck it, what's the worst that can happen," and John laughed out loud. When the SS were involved, there was no limit to the bad things that can happen.

When it was all said and done, John counted 23 women volunteers. He set about arming them first with the guards' nonlethal taser guns and shotguns, then with some of the homemade submachine guns, and various other weapons that they had found in the office. When he was done arming them with helmets, extra boots, and clubs, they looked a little more formidable. While 4 of the HLF crew went about fitting the Farm with timed explosives, Austin, John, and Joy reviewed how to use the various weapons that they had been outfitted with. They didn't have much faith in these new recruits, but they were better than nothing.

"When the time comes, some of them would probably freeze up," thought John. He did see a couple of them that looked ready for battle though, fuck. He could be wrong. If nothing else, after being tortured here, they were probably pissed off enough to hurt someone.

John handed his submachine gun to one of the new recruits. He had outfitted himself with almost all SS weapons, which were more reliable and came with more powerful ammo. He strapped the battle sword and battle knife to his vest, along with the SD Megablaster pistol and his silenced 9mm pistol. He gave Austin the rifle and the 5 magazines. He then examined the latest addition to his arsenal: the MG 42. It weighed about 20 pounds dry, but John found a bunch of belts for it, about 1000 rounds, which made its combined weight about 30 lbs.

John knew that the MG 42 was well worth its weight, as he had used one of them when he was in the Army. That weight came with a price. The MG 42 was nicknamed "The Beast" for a reason: it fucked up both whoever was shot with it, as well as the back of the soldier who had the misfortune to be carrying it on long marches.

Within an hour the Farm was well rigged with explosives. The 77 women prepared to follow the 2 HLF soldiers back through the sewers into another safe house, while the former prisoner volunteers and the 8 of them got themselves ready for the next battle. They would all be entering the sewers, just heading out in different directions.

John, Austin, Joy, and the 5 other HLF soldiers that would be going on the rescue mission fanned out and provided security while the 77 women, led by the HLF soldier guides, went down the ladder. After they were all down the ladder and into the sewers, John and the rest of the group entered. John watched the women, followed by the HLF soldier, who was pulling rear security, leave. It had a feeling of finality to it. Austin broke the silence.

"Ok, huddle up."

The group gathered around, sloshing in the fetid sewer water.

Austin addressed them, trying to sound upbeat.

"Ok, make sure your weapons are loaded, but on safe. You don't want an accidental discharge giving us away or hurting the person in front of you. To our new volunteers, thank you for joining us. Watch what the HLF soldiers are doing and take their lead. All of them have been through a few scrapes and came out on top. Let's not get cocky- we just beat their junior varsity team. I would guess that the Troopers who we are about to fight are going to be much harder, so we are going to have to be sneaky and use surprise. If we do that, maybe, just maybe - some of us will live through it. Good luck everyone."

Austin faked a smile. He didn't think there was any real chance of survival, and, truth be told, he was surprised that they weren't already dead.

CHAPTER 14

Holden rubbed his eyes. He couldn't remember the last time he had slept more than two hours in a row. Each time he let himself drift off to sleep he woke drenched in sweat and wanting to scream. Since he had been forced to join the SS, he felt as though he had been living in a wide-awake nightmare. The violence that he had been forced to commit stuck with him, and it didn't get easier.

When he thought of what he had become, he was beyond himself with grief. What would his mother say if she had seen him bash in that child's skull? What would she have said if she had seen him stab that girl? What would she have said? He wanted to cry. She wouldn't say anything because she had been murdered by the SS.

Last month Holden snuck home to visit his parents. He had been forbidden all contact with his family and figured that they had probably thought the worst when he didn't come home. Holden was surprised to find the family home empty.

Holden searched all over the house for clues where they

had gone, feeling like a low-rent Sherlock Holmes. Though he was thorough, nothing came of the search, and he eventually gave up. Dejected, he returned to his SS barracks with nothing more than a couple of family pictures and lots of questions.

The mystery was solved weeks later. He had been ordered to sort through files of protesters and known rebels. The SS had been trying to find out what the protesters had in common. Was it age, ethnic background, or something else? He started with sorting the files by age, then by gender and then by ethnic background. He concluded that the rebels had come from all walks of life and ethnic backgrounds, and the only thing that bound them was a mistrust of the government and a belief in the sanctity of life.

He was finishing up his assignment and typing up his findings when he was brought the files of rebels from a recent protest to sort through. Most of the files were from people in their 20s, college kids like him. Then he saw the files of his parents. He sat there staring at their names in disbelief. He had imagined that something like this might have happened when he saw the empty house, but he had been holding onto hope that they had just gone on a trip or had moved.

Apparently, his parents had become politically active when Holden had been forcibly inducted into the SS. They had been arrested at a protest and taken into SS custody. The SS usually just bullied the elderly into keeping their mouths shut, but his parents wouldn't be cowed. The file said that his mother had spit in a Trooper's face and his father had told the Commander to go fuck himself.

Obviously, this was something that the Commander couldn't just let go, and he had to make an example of them. Holden read in horror while the file explained how the SS Troopers had raped not only his mom, but his dad as well, and then had burned them both at the stake for being rebels. Reading the file and seeing the attached pictures made him want to vomit, but it was the video of their killings that affected Holden the most.

Images of violence flickered before Holden's tear -filled - eyes. The brutality. The horror. The death. The sorrow. His parents, murdered on video, the laughs of the SS Troopers as the flames consumed his parents, his mother screaming in terror, his father refusing to make a sound despite what must have been excruciating pain. Holden bit his tongue and choked back tears.

Watching their killings brought Holden to the brink of sheer madness, but he needed to see it. He needed to consume the horror and internalize it, for it had ignited in him a near suicidal rage to get revenge for his parents. Before, he had thought that he would do just about anything to survive. Now he realized that living in a world where his parents could be murdered like this was far worse. He vowed that he would watch the Commander die, that the Commander and everyone responsible would pay for what they had done to the world, and that he was willing to forfeit his own life just to make that happen.

CHAPTER 15

After about two hours of trudging through the sewers, Austin gave the signal to halt. He looked at his compass then gestured for them all to huddle up as they had before.

"Ok, this is the spot where we go up. We'll be walking through the woods for the rest of the way there. I want everyone to stay low. Move slowly and try to not make any noise. When we get to the wall, I'll go over first then attach a rope and send it down for the rest of you to climb up. John, could you provide rear security and make sure everyone makes it over the wall?"

John nodded, thinking there was a joke in being rear guard, like "I'll be watching your rear or something," but he let it go. No one was in the mood for his shenanigans.

Austin continued, "I'll be laying down my jacket and some other stuff on top of the wall to cover the barbed wire. Make sure to not knock that off, or it will be quite difficult for the rest of the team to get over the fence without cutting themselves."

Austin surveyed the motley team of veterans and new recruits. Maybe with the element of surprise, maybe, just maybe…He thought to himself. No, we are screwed. Might as well just get hope out of his mind right now.

"Ok. Let's get ready to do this. Check your weapons one last time. They should have a round chambered and be ready to fire, but leave them on safe until you are ready to shoot. Make sure that you know where you are going to grab your first magazine to reload from, and go through the motions of reloading, so it isn't a surprise when you must do it for real. For those with the taser pistols, there really isn't a reloading process. Shoot only if necessary, but hang in the back. We will eventually be able to get you a captured SS Trooper weapon if everything goes well. The first 10 of us out of the hole will take cover behind trees and pull security in a circular clockwork fashion until all of us are safe and above ground. Once we are all out of the sewer, we will move in a "V" formation toward the objective. The name of the game is stealth. Any questions?"

Austin, John, and everyone else looked around but no one seemed to have any questions.

"Ok, let's do this."

As noiselessly as possible, Austin climbed the ladder and

moved the manhole cover back far enough so that even the biggest of them could fit through the hole easily. They filed up the ladder and into the darkness. The night was cold and damp, but at least it wasn't raining. When all of them had emerged from the sewers, they stopped and were as still and as quiet as possible, to see if their exit had been discovered. John thought it was weird that in the quiet, there weren't animal sounds. He knew that they had all died off years ago and that he shouldn't be expecting any, but he still found it strange. He also thought it was weird that there weren't any insects either. He wondered if they were all killed off by the same virus or didn't just want to live in this fucked up world anymore.

Austin gave the signal and they started the slow walk towards the castle. The moonless night provided the cover of darkness to conceal their passage, but the lack of visibility also made walking difficult. The group had to stop a couple of times for stumbles, trips, and a sprained ankle. Luckily, they were able to do all of that without making too much noise and they remained undetected as they approached the castle walls.

John was impressed by Riker's castle. It really DID look

like a castle from the Middle Ages, with steeples and spires straight out of a grade school history lesson. Apparently, some rich asshole had built the castle during a time in history called the "dot- com" boom, where some people had more money than they knew what to do with. Years later, during the reign of President White, Riker had outfitted it to be his own personal fortress. John mused they would probably be able to get over the walls undetected, but would they be able to get to the front door without anyone seeing them? Not likely.

Austin was also impressed by the size of the castle, but something else was more concerning. He noted that there were two guard towers, which he hadn't heard about from the spy network. He imagined that there would be at least one guard in each tower, probably with either a light or heavy machine mounted in it. This development added a layer of difficulty. Austin wondered how they were going to eliminate the guards without waking up the complex. He didn't immediately have an answer, but he determined that if they were able to capture one or both towers then they would have an advantage if they needed to cover their escape in a hurry. Things would probably go south with a quickness.

Austin quietly addressed the group. "Ok, the guard towers are either new or something our spies failed to mention when they cased this place. Either way, we are going to need positive control of them if we are to successfully raid this place."

Austin pointed to two of the veteran HLF soldiers.

"Sara and Jane, you will each take one of the new volunteers with you to watch your back and assault those towers. Sara, you take tower 1 and Jane you take tower 2. Stealth is key, so use your silenced weapons only. Once you have positive control of the towers, reposition those machine guns to face the front of the castle."

Sara and Jane nodded in agreement. They understood the assignment and were tracking.

Austin continued, "The rest of us will be lurking in the shadows. When we see that you have taken the towers, John and I will shoot the guards in front of the castle and then the rest of us will go inside. The main objective is to kill this man, Riker, who I am assuming will be somewhere on the third floor, and to free John's sister and the rest of the prisoners."

"We'll leave the rest of the timed explosives that we are carrying in various parts of the castle, along with some booby traps. Be as quiet as you can until everything goes to shit, then take the silencers off the guns and let them have it."

Austin then pointed to John.

"If everything works as planned, we will have you as the last out of the building, so on your way out you can dump a belt of bullets from your machine gun into whoever is following us. Then run like hell, because Sara and Jane are then going to need us out of the way before they can light up the entire building with their machine guns."

Austin then turned back to Sara and Jane. "Shoot those machine guns dry and arm the explosives to blow in the towers. Then get the hell out of there and don't look back. Meet us back here at the rallying point. We will leave two soldiers at the bottom of the wall to guard our retreat up and over." Austin surveyed the group. "Everyone good?"

They all gave the thumbs up.

John was lost in thought, thinking about all the things that could and would go wrong. He thought about his time in the war and all the missions he had been on. He thought about all the

friends he had lost. He thought about his sister, his family, and his

life. The bad feelings started to come back in waves, but he

stopped them with a single thought. He concluded the only thing

that mattered now was revenge.

"Fuck it," whispered John. "Let's burn this place to the

ground. "

The climb over the castle wall went smoothly. Of course,

it was easier for some than others. The HLF soldiers made quick

work of it while the new volunteers struggled. Still, they were able

to make it over quietly, and they still had the element of surprise.

As luck would have it, the last volunteer before John dislodged

the jacket that was covering the barbed wire, so John's trip over

the wall was bloodier than the rest of them.

John's heavy machine gun made him fall as gracefully as

a bag of cement, and he hit the ground with a grunt of pain. With

maximum effort, he picked himself off the ground. He was full of

cuts and scrapes but was not seriously bleeding.

John slung the MG 42 on his back and took his 9mm

pistol out of his holster. He made sure there was a bullet in the chamber and took the safety off. He was ready for action. Seeing that John was over the fence, Austin led the group towards the towers and along to the front of the building. They lurked in the shadows and luckily didn't come up against any resistance. Then it started to thunder, and rain poured down on them. Austin looked up into the heavens and thanked their good luck. Rain was noisy and would cover the sound they made on the assault. It would almost guarantee the guards would have their hands in their pockets and not on their weapons. The only downside was that it was cold outside, and they would soon be soaked to the bone.

The pairs of women reached the towers about the same time that Austin, John, and the remainder of the team assembled on the side of the building. Austin nodded to Sara and Jane, who started their assent of the tower. John knew that they were to start the assault when the women reached the top of their towers. There was no room for error. They would have to take out the guards quickly and silently or they were all done for.

John looked at the guards. They huddled under the roof, trying to stay out of the rain. He did not feel remorse or pity for them, knowing that they had signed up to protect Riker no matter what evil things he was doing. He understood that in a different situation it might of been him standing guard duty, trying to make his parents and country proud. He noted that the guards were not wearing body armor, probably because they were inside their fence and thought that they would be safe.

John saw the women were soon to be in place and felt a tap on his shoulder from Austin. He stood up, and began walking calmly towards the men, with Austin behind and to his right. He brought the pistol up and placed two shots in quick succession into the first guard's throat and chest. While that guard was busy dying, he shot the next guard twice in the chest.

Austin mowed down the remaining two guards with his silenced submachine gun. He then stopped to listen and survey the scene. Safe for now, nothing but the sound of rain.

Austin looked to the towers and got two thumbs up from Sara and Jane. He gave them a brief second to get the machine guns operational in the towers, and then went through the guards' gear. He found four rifles, five pistols, and a set of keys. Austin had eight of the volunteers discard the taser pistols in favor of more lethal options and made sure they knew not to pull the trigger unless they were trying to kill something. He took the safety off each of them before handing them the guns.

Unfortunately, there would not be enough time for a proper block of instruction in the safe handling of firearms. At this point it was sink or swim, and everyone was neck-deep in water.

CHAPTER 16

The group burst through the castle's ornate double doors, guns up and ready to fire. The entrance to the castle opened to a greeting area with a brightly lit, extravagant grand staircase. Sounds of classical music and smells of cooking and cigar smoke wafted in the air, and expensive-looking portraits of SS leaders hung on the walls. There was almost an old-world party atmosphere. "Good," thought John, "here come the party crashers!"

John steadied his nerves knowing he would have to hold it together and not let his emotions get the best of him. He had to keep thinking rationally and be detached and professional for them to get out of this raid alive. He had to think of this like a video game, except that if he got shot, he wouldn't be able to reset the game and try again.

John and Austin shot two guards as they entered, and the HLF soldiers finished off the rest. The group then stopped and bunched up until they were instructed by Austin to spread out.

They broke into four teams of four, each being led by an

HLF soldier, and each group taking a different floor. John made sure to get the meanest looking volunteers on his team. He whispered to Austin they would be heading towards the fourth floor to where he thought Riker might be. Austin gave his nod of approval. Before they all split up, Austin whispered some final words of instruction.

"Silenced weapons only while we still have the element of surprise. After that, anything goes. Set explosives to blow in 1 hour. Meet down here in 30 minutes. Any questions?"

Austin looked around. Apparently, there weren't any questions, just grim faces that knew it was do-or-die. Austin gave them the thumbs up and smiled a fake smile. "See you all in Valhalla."

John smiled. Valhalla was the Viking kingdom of the dead. To go there, you had to die gloriously in battle. While John didn't believe in God – because how could you believe in a God who would let the world become this shitty – he liked the idea of going to the Viking kingdom in the afterlife. If there was a God, best make him into a badass!

John and his team hit the stairs hard, almost sprinting up

them. The plush royal red carpet dampened their pounding footsteps as they ascended the stairs. Up and up they went, to the first, second, third, and finally, the fourth floor. John wondered where it would end and what they would find when they got there. They still hadn't alerted the entire castle to their presence, and John wondered if they would be able to maintain the element of surprise till the end.

When they finally reached the fourth floor, John motioned for the team to stop and get down low. He peaked around the corner and saw two SS Troopers guarding a huge door. This is what he had been expecting and knew it wouldn't be easy to take them both quietly. He looked at the weapons that his squad had. Only one of them had a silenced weapon, one of the homemade submachine guns. All the other weapons would make too much noise. It was up to him and the new volunteer to take out the guards without making any noise.

He gestured to the volunteer named Marta they would move towards the guards shooting. They were only 10 feet away. John would take the Trooper on the left and Marta would take the Trooper on the right. The Troopers were awake, but they had their rifles slung. If John and Marta hit them with their first couple of shots, they should be ok.

A silent question - "Are you ready?" She nodded yes. Ok, they would go on 3. They counted silently together- "1, 2,..."

On three, they turned the corner and started shooting. Luckily, the castle Troopers weren't wearing body armor and were at a disadvantage when the hail of silenced bullets hit them. John killed his Trooper in 3 shots while Marta emptied her magazine into the Trooper, the wall, the ceiling, the other Trooper, and pretty much everything else in that general direction.

They stopped for a second and waited. No sounds, no sirens, and no alarm bells. Surprising, thought John, as he counted all the bullet holes. He wondered how long their luck was going to hold out. The next room would probably be hard and test them. John readied himself for the worst.

The group moved up to the huge door. It had a key card entrance lock. They took a key card from one of the deceased guards. Easy enough. With a deep breath and guns up, they unlocked the door and entered.

They were in a MASSIVE throne room lit by torch light.

On white marble walls hung magnificent tapestries, probably original works of art from the actual Middle Ages. Gold accented everything, from the crown moldings that lined the walls, to the cups that were in use, to the chandelier that hung from the ceiling. Marble steps in the middle of the room led up to an altar. This white marble altar was adorned with a scarlet cloth and was fitted with human skulls and precious jewels.

Strange music gave the scene an otherworldly, almost surreal, quasi- religious feeling. This was akin to music you might hear at the court in a medieval castle. Across the room, John could see a collection of naked dwarves playing musical instruments. One played a flute, one was singing in a falsetto, one had a tambourine and drums, and the last one was playing a stringed instrument that John mistakenly thought was a guitar, but was actually a lute.

Naked women were chained all around the room. Walls were decorated by trophies made from preserved decapitated heads of beautiful women. The decapitated heads were all arranged so that it appeared that they were staring straight at the action in middle of the throne room.

Riker was busy raping John's sister on the altar. She was held down by two naked women. Far from being mere spectators in the rape, the women were taking an active role. They put their fingers in her while they smiled and laughed. They kissed each other and they spat on her and then congratulated Riker on a job well done. An armed male SS Trooper stood off to the side, enjoying the spectacle.

John was wondering how the SS was able to get all these women to submit to this sickness. Closer examination of the women gave him some clues. The two women who were helping with the rape of John's sister had SS blood type tattoos, the kind of tattoo that Troopers received after their basic training. This meant that they were an active part of this fucked up mess.

Most of the other women had things taped to their arms, which John recognized to be IV access. A topless SS woman made the rounds with a syringe, injecting a clear liquid into all the chained-up women's IV ports. John watched as the prisoners would thrash about, trying in vain to avoid the injection. and then go into a daze once the solution was administered. By the moaning and the dilated pupils, John guessed the women were being drugged with morphine and maybe even ketamine, which would explain the complacent nature of the prisoners.

A large SS Trooper stirred a mysterious green soup in a large cauldron off to the side of the altar. After stirring the strange brew, he ladled some of it into a bowl for one of the other SS Troopers. In the middle of bowl was an eyeball. John could see various body parts in the cauldron floating around: arms, legs, heads, and even genitals.

The team spread out and got into position, and on John's signal, they opened a can of whoop-ass. John's first bullets hit the two female SS Troopers in the chest and stomach and grazed Riker in the head, taking off his ear and causing him to let out a yell. The HLF fighters shot the two male SS Troopers, and they slumped to the ground, mortally wounded.

Riker jumped to his chair and pushed a button triggering an alarm, which blasted loudly. John calmly instructed the volunteers to free the chained women and try to find them some clothes, and to set the timed explosives. They would be leaving shortly.

John and Riker's eyes met, and for a brief second it

looked like Riker was going to surrender. Riker suddenly went for his pistol, but before he could get off a shot, John whipped out his battle sword and cut off Riker's hand. Riker let out a howl and clutched his stump, blood spraying everywhere. A bloodied SS Trooper got in his path, but John booted her out of the way.

John stared at Riker, and Riker smiled at him.

"No matter what happens to me, you won't leave my castle in one piece," cackled Riker.

John smiled. "Challenge accepted."

The battle sword hummed with life, screaming for bloodshed. John sliced off Riker's arms in two quick cuts, and just as Riker was starting to let out a scream, John moved in for the final blow, the finishing move, the show- stopper.

With all his might, John struck Riker on the head, going right through his skull and into his torso and out his groin. The sword didn't stop until it clanged on the ground. Blood gushed everywhere. The many pieces of the man that was formerly known as Riker lay in a heap of blood and guts, along with the dying SS Troopers.

John surveyed his handiwork and with a satisfied flick of

the wrist, removed the blood from the sword. The sword went back into the sheath and out came the MG 42. With a click- clack John engaged the charging handle and made the gun lethal. He turned to the group of volunteers and the women they had just rescued, most of which looked like they were going to be sick. He hugged his sister, who by this point had been clothed by the volunteers. Gloria was obviously still in shock and crying.

"Let's get THE FUCK out of here!" roared John.

They opened the door and were instantly met by gunfire. Two of the rescued women went down. John and the volunteers returned fire. The sound of the gunfire in the hallway was deafening

After a couple of exchanges of gunfire John saw that they had taken out their targets. He gestured that they were leaving. The group nodded back. It was time to GO!

The surviving members of the group advanced through the open door guns drawn. When they got to the steps they were again met by gunfire, but John mowed them down with a quick spray of machine gun fire from the MG 42. When John was in infantry training back in the day, he had learned that the proper amount of time to hold down the trigger of a machine gun was the amount of time it took to say, "Killing a family of seven." Surveying the damage, he reckoned that he had only killed a family of 5, and it had taken him 20 shots to do it. "Sloppy, sloppy," thought John as he changed machine gun belts in his gun. Click- clack, and John's gun was ready to rock and roll again.

The team turned the corner. One of the volunteers took a bullet in the arm and let out a shriek as she sent a magazine of bullets flying off in every direction. When John looked over to see the woman get hit, he missed the SS Trooper coming straight for them.

The Trooper leveled his gun at the group and shot them at point-blank range. John was hit in the arm. As he turned, he watched in slow- motion as the Trooper sprayed the rest of the team with hot lead. Oblivious to his own pain, John ran over to check on the wounded. He realized with horror that his own sister was among the dead and dying.

John had just a moment to hold his dying sister before she passed. She looked up at him, blood pouring from her nose and mouth. Gloria tried to speak, but all that came out was a bloody, gurgled, garbled mess. She reached up and put a bloody hand on John's face and then she was gone. John thought of the irony of the situation – he had tried to save his sister, only to have gotten her killed. He wished, in that moment, that he had died instead.

John got to his feet and turned to face the SS Trooper. The man was fumbling with a magazine change, which bought the stunned group the time they needed to react. Through his tears, John watched his hands turn his machine gun towards the Trooper. The machine gun erupted into violence, spraying the Trooper with bullets. The man dropped to the ground; his body torn in half by the machine gun fire. John spat in the dying man's face and kicked him once in the side for good measure.

The group moved down the stairs cautiously. They were almost to the entrance way where they would meet up with the rest of the team and make their exit. John didn't want to get his hopes up, knowing all too well that this wasn't going to be easy. His fears were well-founded, for when they got to the bottom of the steps, SS Troopers began to pour out of every door. Austin and his group returned, guns blazing.

'What took you so long? Where's your sister?" asked Austin.

John didn't answer, but the look on his face told Austin she didn't make it.

One of the other groups returned, but two of their members were gunned down just as they arrived. By this time, all but one of the women that they had rescued from the throne room had been killed, and most of the team had been shot at least once. John thought about how lucky they had been to this point. The fact that any of them were still alive was nothing short of a miracle.

"How long are we going to wait for the other group?" whispered John, knowing that it was unnecessary to whisper, but he was doing it anyway.

As if to answer, Austin's watch beeped - 30 minutes had gone by. Austin turned to the rest of the group and made a circling motion with his right hand. It was time to go!

They ran out the front door and John turned to burn a final machine gun belt into their pursuers. He fired his machine gun from the hip this time, spitting lead and death into their enemies. The sound of bullets flying, ricochets and glass breaking was ear-shattering. John was about half – deaf from his time in the Army so it didn't bother him as much as it would have a "normal" person.

When the gun was dry, he pulled a quick release lever on the weapon's sling which sent the bulky MG 42 clattering to the ground. His pistol immediately came up and he delivered three more Troopers to an early grave before he turned and fled. Right on cue, after John was out of the way, the towers opened up with machine gunfire and bullets rained down on the castle entrance. Dozens of Troopers that were following the survivors were shot to pieces.

The women that were in the towers quickly descended and joined the fleeing group. One of the HLF soldiers had twisted her ankle coming down the final ladders and was doing an admirable job of limping at a fast rate to keep up with the rest of them. John took her submachine gun so she could concentrate on the walking process. She handed him her two spare magazines without saying a word and started booking, along with the other women.

John turned to provide cover for their exit. He sprayed the first magazine without trying to hit anything, just to keep the enemies' heads down. He took his time and fired more controlled pairs with the second magazine, aiming at targets and watching his breathing so he was able to do the most damage with his shot groups. This time, he was able to clip a few of the pursuers, some of them more than once. Once the submachine clacked that it was out of ammo, John dropped it on the ground and started running at full speed.

It took all of John's self-control to concentrate on the mission at hand and to not let despair get the better of him. He had just rescued his sister only to watch her die. He was going to be haunted by those images for the rest of his life. How was he going to explain this to his parents? Speaking of his parents, would he ever see them again? Was all the sacrifice worth it? How would they possibly outrun the government, even if they did escape today? He choked back tears of worry, stress, and sadness.

"No time for that shit now," he mumbled to himself.

Two HLF soldiers were pulling guard duty when he reached the wall. He turned around to see how close the stragglers were to joining the group, just in time to see them get gunned down by SS Troopers.

"Fuck," he thought, as he turned to go over the wall.

John followed the survivors through the woods and back into the sewers. Of the 20 that had started on this mission, only 10 remained. "Not good, not good at all," thought John. If there is safety in numbers, then this shit was getting un-fucking safe. He looked down at his bleeding arm, making a mental note that he would have to put a bandage on it once they stopped to catch their breath.

John came out of his thoughts when they got to the sewer manhole cover. He pulled security as Austin led the group down the hole. John was the last one through, and pulled the cover shut.

John dropped to the ground, splashing in the dirty water. He was careful to not get any of it on the arm that had the bullet hole in it. John was pretty sure the HLF's resources didn't include antibiotics and medical care.

The group trudged through the sewers for hours until Austin led them to another secret hideout bunker. Austin saw

John's surprised face and laughed.

"We have 100s of these safe houses all over the country," Austin said.

Joy bandaged John's arm and they all were given food and drink. There wasn't a bathroom, but designated male and female parts of the sewer to go do their business in. Luckily, one of the things that the HLF had stocked in the bunker, besides emergency rations, guns, ammo, and water, was toilet paper. John took a roll of toilet paper and went to relieve himself. While he would have preferred a clean, comfortable toilet like the one back home, this worked just as well.

CHAPTER 17

The Commander got a call that his presence had been requested in the Research and Development Labs. The Commander smiled from ear to ear. He loved going to the R&D Labs. Science and mathematics had been his favorite subjects as a child, and the combination of science and violence was just his thing. He loved the feeling of amazement and awe, walking through the aisles of experimental weapons at the labs. It was like being a kid in a toy store. No, he thought. Not just any toy store. It was like being at Santa Claus's North Pole workshop.

The Commander left his office and walked down the long hallways of the SS HQ building, past the rows of cubicles of civil servants and office workers that made the SS possible. The neatness of the offices and the clean, well-maintained building that was the SS HQ always made him happy. He started to whistle a tune.

The R&D Labs were in a gigantic industrial- looking building about 100 feet away from the main SS HQ building. It could be reached through an underground access tunnel, but the

Commander preferred to go outside and see the gardens and manicured shrubbery that were on either side of the walkway. The Commander loved to smell the flowers, to memorize their Latin names, and put them in a flower press to savor later. He thought with a laugh, that sometimes he also collected his victim's heads, and that in a way, he enjoyed collecting them much in the same way as the flowers.

He reached the door to the building and was checked by security. The Troopers who were guarding the doors knew who he was but had to check his credentials and scan his ID anyway. There would be no lax in security, even for a known official, and the Troopers knew all too well that they would have been severely punished if they had just let the Commander through without making him go through all the security protocols.

The Commander looked at the directory and thought of all the wonderful things that the SS were doing in this building. On the first floor they were working towards curing cancer by conducting experiments with live human volunteers. They would give the "volunteers" cancer, then experiment with various treatments until all the volunteers died. On the second floor they were experimenting with saving trauma victims by creating trauma in volunteers and then working out new ways to save lives. The third floor housed the computer and technological advances, such as the implanted biotech devices and internet mind control. The fourth floor housed the bureaucrats and the technocrats. Paper pushers. So necessary and yet, so boring.

The Military Technology Lab (MTL) was in the bottom of the building. It housed the most classified secrets of the SS and was not listed in the directory. Entrance was restricted and the experiments there were top secret. The Commander pressed the button on the elevator for B5 and scanned his badge. He entered the elevator and prepared himself for the 5-minute descent into the very bowels of the building. He started to hum a tune to pass the time.

The MTL was buzzing with activity. Hundreds of scientists were busy creating new weapons and gear in a space that looked big enough to comfortably house a football stadium. The aisles were very wide so forklifts could move the tanks, robotics, and weaponry easily from point A to point B. The hustle and bustle of activity and the hydraulic whine of machinery was loud, and almost hard to talk over, let alone think over. The Commander smiled, thinking about how much he loved watching all this creativity.

The Commander wondered what new creation he was going to be shown today. Would it finally be a laser gun capable of killing someone with a single beam of light? Would it be an improved battle sword that could cut through steel as quickly as it did human bones? Would it be a nuclear grenade? A new tank capable of underwater travel, perhaps. Oh, the possibilities were endless, and the thought of each one made the Commander happy. No matter what it was, he was sure it was going to be awesome.

A man dressed in a lab coat introduced himself as the lead scientist of PROJECT MK ULTRA and lead the way through the aisles to the assembly room. Once inside the room the noise of the Research and Development was barely audible, and with the door shut, it was as quiet as a tomb. The COMMANDER marveled at how well the room had been constructed to have made it completely soundproof. He was also thankful the air conditioning system worked.

The lights in the room dimmed, and the scientist who had led the Commander into the room addressed the crowd:

"Friends, colleagues, and distinguished guests from the government, the SS, as well as from private industry and from local policing, thank you very much for coming. It is with much hope for a prosperous and safe future together that I have the honor to present to you the fruit of 5 years of labor- PROJECT MK ULTRA!"

A curtain went up and a spotlight went to the stage behind the speaker. There was loud, flashy music and a lead up to the big reveal. The curtain went up and out walked an SS Trooper. The uniform didn't appear to be any different from other Troopers, other than having a gigantic eagle painted on the breastplate of the armor. A buzz went through the audience. The Commander, on the other hand, was unimpressed. What the fuck was this?

The scientist surveyed the audience and could see from the faces that he was going to have to sell his invention better than this.

"Ladies and gentlemen, what is the most important

instrument of war? Is it the sword? Is it the gun? Is it the tank? Perhaps the bomb?"

The scientist looked around and smiled.

"No, I would argue that the most important instrument of war is the soldier himself. For thousands of years men have fought and died and while the weapons have been upgraded from bows and arrows to machine guns, the fighting has always been the same. Until now."

"With PROJECT MK ULTRA -short for "MASTER KILLER" ULTRA - we have upgraded the abilities of soldiers. These new suits are up- armored to be impervious to small arms fire and can withstand the blast from a grenade. They are fireproof and contain an internal bladder of oxygen in a closed system that can allow the wearer to be underwater or in a room with toxic gas for up to 2 hours without negative effects."

The scientist clapped his hands, and electronic music started pumping through the speakers. Assistants wheeled various things out on the stage to demonstrate what the suit could do. The Trooper punched through cinder blocks and then tank armor. He lifted a car over his head. He took blaster pistol fire directly to the helmet and then sat fully immersed in water for twenty minutes. He walked through a wall of fire and was hit with a sledgehammer in the groin. All of this had seemingly no effect on the wearer.

The scientist continued.

"While all this is an incredible leap in safety for our Troopers, the real game changer is the built-in robotic assist strength enhancer. What can a normal man bench? Our average Trooper can bench 200 or so pounds, and some of the above average men can do 300, or even 400 lbs. With the robotic assist technology of these suits, even the weakest of our troopers will be able to easily manage 10,000 lbs. That's not all the strength assist is good for. This suit will allow the wearer to punch through concrete walls, pick up cars, and do some truly amazing things. Our Troopers will no longer be only soldiers. They will be gods among men."

The scientist clapped his hands and electronic music started playing through the speakers. The music was meant to pump up the audience, but the Commander didn't need to be convinced of the merits of the new devices. He was already sold.

He had visions of his Troopers walking through mobs of HLF fighters, slaughtering them by the hundreds. In the past few weeks, the incidents at the Dairy Farm and Riker's Castle had been embarrassments, but with the help of these suits he would unleash a TERROR of epic proportions on their enemies. The streets would run red with blood, and the cruelty and violence would make the creator himself sick.

CHAPTER 18

John, Austin, and the rest of the HLF soldiers sat around the sewer bunker for about a month. In that space of time, they went from just being happy to be alive to being stir crazy. Some of them even started to wonder if they would be better off taking their chances fighting it out with the SS in the world above. Austin received word through a coded message on an old radio in the bunker. The SS had issued orders for a nationwide manhunt for them. If they were caught, they would be executed as terrorists, or put up on a mock trial, tortured and humiliated in front of the whole world, and then slowly murdered. Either way, the situation was bleak.

John was burning in his own private hell. All the danger and the possibility of dying in the raid would have been worth it if he had saved his sister. Instead, she had died, as had many other good people that day. Sure, he had killed Riker, and they had destroyed Riker's Castle, but what was John going to tell his parents when he saw them? How was he going to explain that he got Gloria killed, and that her body was blown to bits along with the rest of the castle? In the moment, REVENGE had felt sweet, but it was only empty calories. Now, all John was left with was a feeling of sadness and regret.

After a meeting one day, John told Joy the story of how he had gotten involved with HLF in the first place. He had joined the HLF to save his sister and had only succeeded in getting her killed. He told her that the guilt was eating him alive. "Why did she have to die," asked John, tears in his eyes. There wasn't much that Joy could say, but the hug did help.

Joy then opened up to John about her involvement in the group. Joy had been a member of the HLF since she was a teenager. Her family had started off going to protests while they were still legal and had gone underground and off the grid with the group when the government enacted Project Carnivore. Her father had been killed in one of the group's first raids (called "Direct Action") years ago, when the poorly armed rebels attempted to overcome one of the SS outposts.

Two years later her mother was captured by the SS during a "Direct Action" and sent to the Dairy Farm and was never heard from again. Now, Joy could only see her parents in her dreams and longed to be with them again, far away from this wide-awake nightmare.

Technically, Joy outranked John in the HLF since she had been with the organization for years, whereas John had just been thrown into the group recently. John made sure to address her as ma'am every chance he got, and that made her smile. Joy laughed at the absurdity of the greeting, given their age differences and the fact that John had led men into combat before. Joy felt confident enough to take care of herself, but to lead people on missions was another thing all together.

John was so caught up in his grief he didn't initially notice that Joy had started to flirt with him. "Flirting" started off small. A raised eyebrow here and there. They would sneak glances at each other during meetings, looking away when they were noticed. This escalated into them "accidentally" bumping into each other while doing tasks around the hideout, always finding a reason to be where they thought the other might be.

At first, he wrote it off as her just pretending to like him to be nice, but as the days went on, he got the feeling that she was interested in him. Joy was cute and had her shit together, arguably even more so than John. "Women always have their shit together more than men," thought John.

John didn't think that there was any point to it. It's not like the world was going to UNFUCK itself anytime soon, so there would never be a chance of "normal" dates, or any of the other things that John remembered enjoying from the whole "courting" experience before the world changed. Still, it DID pass the time, and it DID give him something else to think about besides his survivor guilt.

Things changed for them one night. Joy had gone to one of the rooms that they were using as a bathhouse to clean up. John happened to be on watch, patrolling the sewers. He stopped by the bathhouse, innocently knocking to check on her. She answered and told him to come in.

He opened the door and found her standing there naked, except for her combat boots. Joy was 5'5" and her tan skin glistened in the light. Her eyes sparkled with a youthful mischievous innocence.

"See anything you like?" she asked playfully. He smiled, taking in the sights.

"Sure," he said, almost a little overwhelmed.

He embraced her and was surprised to discover she was warm, as it was chilly in the sewers. He leaned in for a kiss and his mouth found hers. It was a great kiss: gentle, with just enough passion and saliva exchanged to register as fulfilling without overdoing it. Both of them ignored the fact they probably should have brushed their teeth before kissing.

John gently caressed her. Joy's feedback was instantaneous. Based on her positive reaction, John figured that he was doing something right. It had been a while since John had been this close to a naked woman, and he didn't want to mess it up. They stood there in the middle of the bathhouse kissing and caressing for what seemed like ages, until Joy led him to a corner of the bathhouse. She laid her bath towel down, and took his hand, leading him down on top of her.

They laid there kissing for a while, and then John's mouth travelled all over her, kissing her breasts, her navel, and then going for a trip south of the border. John tasted her. The salty, gooey flavor made him smile, in the same way sampling an ice cream flavor from your childhood might. He continued for some time, until he could tell that she made it to the place of the clouds and rain.

She opened her eyes, grabbed him by the hair and said, "Now I want you in me."

John laughed, taking off his shirt. "Well, ma'am, it looks like you know what you want."

John was especially amazed by the way that she squatted down on him while she was on top, riding him in a way that asserted her dominance of the situation. She rode him as a modern-day cowgirl would use a mechanical bull, showing off to friends.

She then got on all fours, turning to John, and mimicked panting like a dog.

John smiled, both because he missed dogs and because he liked having sex in this position.

They finished face to face missionary style, locked in a desperate embrace, not wanting the magic of the lustful moment to end, because in it at least they had each other and they were not alone.

When it was over, she leaned over and kissed him.

"Well?" she said.

"Well, what?" He answered.

She punched him playfully on the arm. "Well, what do you think?" She asked.

He looked up at the sewer's ceiling, stretching out an arm to bring her in tight.

"Well, I mean, it's my first-time having sex in a sewer, but it was pretty good, I guess. I suppose I would do it again," he said, teasing her.

"Oh, would you, huh?" she joked.

"Yes, I would. Also, I must give you points for your outfit. Naked except for combat boots?"

They laid there curled up together talking for a while, caressing each other and pretending that they weren't scared about losing each other. In this world, they had already lost so much, and losing each other now would be too much to bear.

CHAPTER 19

One day Austin called the group together. He had a lot of news to share. The team was all ears. They were ready for a change, eager to do something besides eat rice, sleep, and look for a new place in the sewer to take a shit.

"Ok, here's the deal. Yes, they are still looking for us. Yes, they have been executing prisoners on TV, and yes, if we sat here for years hiding out, they would eventually find us. This is the government that we are talking about. They find everyone eventually, but they aren't going to find us because we are going to go looking for them instead."

The team looked around puzzled. What could he possibly mean by that?

"You are probably wondering what I mean by that," Austin continued, sensing the question. "Well, it's simple. While we wait, the enemy gets stronger. So, instead of waiting for them to come to us, we are going to bring the fight to them. We are going to hit them hard again. Remember what the best defense is?!"

Austin waited for a reply, looking around the room. No one said anything.

John sighed. "A good offense?"

Austin, feeling validated, finished his sales pitch. "Like last time, we will take volunteers from the women that we've rescued, to augment our group, and strike them hard. Unlike last time, though, we are going to hit a slaughterhouse. If we can rescue some of those guys, we are going to have a bunch of pissed off people that will be more than willing to help us fight. Who's with me?"

Austin looked around to see some less than enthusiastic faces. John was the one that spoke and said what was on everyone's minds.

"I mean, we are with you. What else are we going to do? We are just hoping that there is a solid plan this time. They had no idea that we were attacking last time, and we still lost more than half of our group. I would be willing to believe the guards will have doubled if not tripled everywhere. Unlike the Dairy Farm, they will all be heavily ARMED and wearing body ARMOR! None of us are afraid to die. We just want to make sure that it counts for something. We will probably only get one chance to hit this slaughterhouse, so we are going to need to get this right the first time."

Austin looked around the room. He saw the nods of agreement. He saw the strength in their eyes, their passion for freedom, and their determination to fight on, despite the hopelessness of their situation.

"I understand how you feel. A lot has been asked from you, and I wish that I could tell you it is going to get better. I wish I could, but I can't. Shit is going to get worse before it gets better, and it is going to take a lot of blood to wash away these sins."

"I've talked to the other regional HLF chapters. What we are going to do is move to a local safe house, outfit, and strike. We are going to link up with another local unit and should have a combined 30 soldiers before we move out."

John was surprised. "I had no idea that there were other groups! I thought it was just us!"

"The HLF is much bigger than just our group, "Austin replied. "Chapters are popping up all over the country. We are all autonomous cells, so if any one group gets raided, we can't disclose the locations of the others. The Human Agriculture Industry is on the ropes. The problem is, as long as people are still paying for meat instead of just eating plants, there will always be a demand for human flesh, and the cycle of death will continue. It's very discouraging that people just can't seem to understand the connection between the dead meat on their plates and the suffering they are causing. While the government is corrupt and protects the companies that destroy our planet and murders people by the millions, the real villains are the people who know better and yet refuse to change. The government just backs their plays."

Austin waited for that to sink in, and then continued, "So here's the plan: we pack up and leave at dawn, and head towards the safe house in District 13. We'll be traveling through the sewers. The journey will take about two days. We won't be coming back here, so don't leave anything of value behind. Destroy anything with personal information on it like names, addresses, or anything that might identify any of us. When we get there, we will link up that group, re-arm, and plan for a full-scale raid of the Happy Times Slaughterhouse. Reports have shown there might be as many as 500 people being processed on any given day. That's a lot of lives hanging in the balance, counting on the success of this mission. I promise you, this time we will have a plan before we show up, not just wing it. There are too many people involved for that."

The group packed up their things and got their gear ready for the next day's journey. John laid out his gear on his blanket, did an inventory, and made sure that everything was in good working order. He cleaned all his weapons, disassembling, and reassembling all of them. After asking around, he secured 3 magazines for the submachine gun along with a silencer. He looked over the combat vest he had taken from an SS Trooper. The vest would provide an easy way to carry the magazines along with providing protection from most bullets. He had the SD Megablaster, which he still hadn't fired, along with one spare magazine for it. He was down to half a mag in his 9mm pistol and was surprised that it hadn't jammed after all the rounds that he put through it. He made sure that he got a couple of extra magazines for it as well.

Lastly, he looked over the battle sword and battle knife,

which were way fucking cool and worth the extra weight. Since he had sliced all the way through Riker, he wondered if he could make it through two people with just one swing. He also thought that what he did to Riker reminded him of how people used to do the same thing to animals, just because they wanted to eat them. He shook his head, lost in thought. The world was indeed a strange place, and it didn't always make sense.

The long walk was not without its perils. On the first day alone, there were two sprained ankles, which slowed the march down considerably. Austin banged his nose when he slipped and face planted into the dirty sewer water. This caused him no harm, but he looked rather silly. John didn't have any slips or trips but suffered from back pain as a result of his years of carrying a heavy rucksack while in the Army. The miles wore on him. Part of him wished the walk would be over soon, but he remembered the adage that he should be careful about what he wished for, because it might just come true.

The night before had been difficult for all of them. It was normally hard to sleep in the sewer, but the shared feeling of anxiety of the upcoming mission amplified that. Everyone tossed and turned, was startled by every sound, and annoyed by Mary, who COULD sleep through anything and snored very, very loudly to prove it. The snoring especially bothered John, who was a light sleeper.

As they ended their first day of walking, they started to get worn out and let their guards down. John knew it was happening, but his lack of sleep had made him drop his guard. He was exhausted, trudging along with face and gun down and not paying as much attention as he should have, given the fact that he was at the head of the group. He turned the corner and literally walked right into an SS scout. The two men stumbled backwards, almost falling into the muck of the dirty sewer.

John and the scout stared at each other for a brief second, unsure of what to do. The scout's weapon was slung on his back and John's submachine gun was out, but held low. The man fumbled for his pistol and John watched him do so for what felt like seasons. John finally came out of his daze and shot him twice in the chest at point-blank range.

John turned to give Austin the "where the fuck did that guy come from?" look before he walked over and put a final silenced shot into the man's skull. John took the dead man's slung XVX 10 FURY Battle Rifle from him, along with the spare magazines that he was carrying. Upon going through his clothing, he found a map revealing the locations of many of the HLF safe houses. The whole group was taken aback. Where did their information come from? Was there yet another spy in their midst, and if so, how would they figure out who it was?

Austin quickly addressed the group, "This scout could very well be part of a bigger hunting party of SS Troopers. We got seriously lucky with this one. I know of a hideout not on the scout's map. We'll go rest there for the night."

It was good that Austin knew of a safe spot to hide. It was also good that he purposely failed to mention that the hideout would be 5 miles out of their way, because if the group knew, it would have broken their spirits. All were exhausted and most fell asleep immediately when they arrived. Mary didn't keep anyone awake this time, and Austin was somewhat amused by the awful snoring noise as he kept watch. Eventually, he traded places with John and was able to get some much-needed sleep.

CHAPTER 20

In the early morning, the group awoke and finished the long march to their destination. They trudged for hours through the dirty sewers, and when they finally reached the objective, they were all exhausted. It was then that Austin revealed that the safe house was in the middle of a small, abandoned town, and that they would have to wait another couple of hours until nightfall, when they could safely leave the sewers under the cover of darkness. They found a somewhat dry, but still uncomfortable spot, to make a temporary camp until it was time to make the move.

Austin woke the group up after 4 hours of restless napping. No one was well rested, but everyone was excited to leave the sewers and be done with this forced march. Austin explained that they would be exiting the sewer in teams of two, taking cover where they could find it, and moving as slowly and as quietly as possible. The objective was not to reach the destination as quickly as they could, but in one piece without alerting anyone to their presence. They had no idea what forces might be patrolling the city, and they wanted to keep their heads low.

The group exited the sewer in pairs of two as planned, staying low and getting behind whatever cover they could find. When the entire team was out of the sewer, they replaced the manhole cover and slowly made their way through the deserted town towards the safe house. They traveled under the cover of darkness, stopping every time someone thought they heard a noise. Every shadow was a possible enemy, and every bump in the night a possible threat.

"Better safe than sorry," thought John. He was surprised that they were still alive, and occasionally entertained the fantasy that somehow, someway, he could make it through this whole ordeal and still have a life after this. He would love to see his mom and dad again and tell them all about his adventures. Maybe he could even have a family of his own someday. Pictures of a possible future danced in his brain – maybe even with Joy - and he entertained the images for a brief second before he dismissed them as the fiction that they were. He was going to fight like hell, but he knew that he had to stay focused on the mission, and not on these fantasies.

The slow-moving column made its way through the town until at long last they reached the safe house. The secret knock was made, along with the challenge and password. The HLF SOP (Standard Operating Procedure) was to always assume that their code had been hacked, so even when everything was done correctly, the group was still greeted with guns in their faces. They had all learned the hard way that it was better to be safe than sorry.

The Lincoln Chapter of the HLF welcomed them to the safe house and gave them a quick tour, showed them what they had for food, and directed them to where sleeping and shitting would happen. Austin mentioned the upcoming planned attack on the slaughterhouse, and their leader, Steve, said that they were all in, down to the last fighter. That would make a total of 30 HLF fighters for the liberation raid. Austin mentioned that he thought there were more warriors for the raid.

"KIA (Killed In Action)," lamented Steve. "We hit another target last week, and we suffered some heavy losses. A lot of guys got killed, and we lost a lot of our guns. The SS probably thinks they are winning, and they aren't wrong. Where they ARE wrong is that they expect us to hide. The reason that I said yes to the slaughterhouse mission is that we need your help with another mission first. If all goes as planned, we should be able to even the score with these SS bastards."

"What do you have in mind?" asked Austin.

CHAPTER 21

A tip had come through to SS Headquarters as to the location of one of the HLF safe houses. After looking up the location on the map and verifying the information through various networks, the Commander assembled a platoon of Troopers and his own 5- man personal security detail to go check it out. The men were equipped with MG 42 machine guns, blaster rifles, blaster pistols, rocket launchers, and of course, FLAMETHROWERS. They had enough firepower to kill a small city and were not worried about a few rebels.

They arrived at the remote cabin in the middle of the night. The Commander had them observe light and noise discipline to not give away their location. Quietly, they staked out the cabin. So far, no noise. There was nothing to be heard except the occasional gust of wind. They watched and listened.

They waited for two hours, and still, nothing happened– no sounds, no light, no movement in the cabin. The Commander had first squad get ready to move in, third squad set up to do overwatch with the MG 42 machine guns, and second squad ready to move in as first squad's backup.

First squad quietly moved on the cabin. The heavily armed professional killers confidently walked deliberately and methodically up the path, looking for threats and readying to level deadly violence on whomever came into their gun sights. They were sure that they had the upper hand in this conflict and would prevail once they found the HLF.

What the SS Troopers didn't know was that they were walking into an ambush. The HLF had been planning the attack for weeks, and Austin himself had called in the "tip." The movement that the SS informants had verified had been the HLF setting up fortified firing positions with machine guns, landmines, tripwires, and booby traps.

First squad confidently crept forward like hunters ready to fall on their prey. As they approached the cabin, machine gun fire suddenly erupted and strafed the men, cutting the first three down instantly. The remaining two turned to flee but they stumbled over a tripwire in their haste to escape and set off booby traps. The Troopers exploded into a pile of random limbs and bloody mush.

The Commander and the SS Troopers were shocked. What had just happened? They were so confident of their victory that they had already cashed the check. Then a man to the Commander's right exploded when a sniper's bullet hit him in the head. His blood and brains splattered the Commander in the face.

The Commander calmly wiped the blood and bits of brain from his eyes and turned to his communication expert.

"Radio for backup. We have underestimated the enemy."

The HLF sniper took out a second and then a third Trooper. The HLF sniper was lying 300 feet from the ambush using a SPARTAN .50 caliber semi-automatic sniper rifle with a 30x scope. Both him and his spotter had night vision goggles and knew exactly where they were firing. There was an identical sniper hide set up with views on the other side. When the Commander sent in second squad, the snipers took out the lead man before he was even able to approach the house. HLF machine guns opened on the Troopers, but this time, third squad moved their machine guns into a better position. They dumped 100s of rounds into the house. The sound of gunfire was deafening.

Austin had prepared for this eventuality. The machine

guns were set up in sandbag bunkers inside the cabin that insulated them from the enemy machine gun fire. The HLF machine gunners waited until the firing had stopped, crouching for dear life behind the sandbags. When it stopped, they sat up and returned fire, taking out some of third squad's machine gunners and part of the approaching second squad as well.

While morale was very high among the HLF soldiers, they knew the plan was to not stay and fight it out with the SS, but to leave before the reinforcements arrived. When push came to shove, the HLF soldiers knew that they would not be able to go toe-to-toe with the SS. Their main objective was to take out as many SS Troopers as possible without getting hurt themselves. If the snipers could kill the Commander, that would be even better, but it wasn't worth getting themselves killed.

The Commander sent a final wave of Troopers against the cabin. The Commander's motivation was to try to capture an HLF soldier alive so he could get them to talk. Predictably, the machine guns cut the advancing Troopers apart, while a sniper's bullet claimed the life of yet another of the Commander's bodyguards.

Then the cavalry arrived; one hundred heavily armed Troopers, a tank, and a helicopter. They set up spotlights all around the cabin. The Commander got on the loudspeaker and addressed the rebels.

"Worthy adversaries! Congratulations on a game well-played. You have kept us at bay for two hours. We have thrown everything we have at you, and you have stood your ground. You should be proud of your achievement and all that you have accomplished today. However, this is where we stop playing this game of cat and mouse. As you know, the mouse never wins this game, and we are ready to pounce."

His men looked at each other, and then one of them spoke. "Sir, do cats and mice play? I mean, when they used to be alive? I thought they hated each other and didn't play any games."

The Commander rolled his eyes and promised to explain the metaphor to them later and got back on the loudspeaker.

"Ok, I'm going to give you to the count of three. If you don't give up by then, we will pounce, and you will all die. I can't promise you clemency, but I can at least promise you a fair trial."

The Commander's men looked at each other. They all

knew it was a lie and were surprised the Commander would stoop to telling lies like that. He was known for being straightforward and brutal, which his men respected about him.

"Ok, last chance. One…two…three…."

They waited breathlessly. No movement. Not a sound. Were the HLF just going to sit there and wait for them to come get them?

The Commander gave the word to begin. Instantly, a barrage of machine gun fire, rockets, and mortars rained down on the cabin. The firing and explosions lit up the sky and made it look like the long forgotten American holiday, the 4th of July. The Commander savored the fireworks, thinking of his childhood and days of innocence. After about 5 minutes of hell, he smiled and said, "Ok, that should be enough, cease fire."

This time, the Commander wasn't taking any chances. He sent the tank in. The tank bulldozed the cabin, reducing it to rubble. When the tank was done driving over the ruins, and the Commander was confident that no one was left alive, he sent in a team of ten Troopers.

The Troopers confirmed that there was nothing left alive

in the building. Then, kicking around the ruins, they found a trap door. The Troopers excitedly radioed the find back to the Commander. The Commander yelled at them to not open the door, but he was too late. One of the men opened it. The last thing those Troopers heard before they were all blown to smithereens was an ominous "click."

Standing in the distance, the Commander watched his men blow themselves up with amusement. He said not to open that trap door, and what did they do? They opened the trap door. He thought with amusement that this round goes to the HLF.

"Oh well," he said. "Curiosity got the cat."

The men looked at each other puzzled. Here he goes again talking about extinct animals.

The HLF team retreated into the mountains. Spirits were high and their morale had been boosted. The operation had been a success, but they wouldn't get lucky forever, thought Austin. They were outgunned and outmanned. The SS had an endless supply of troops and guns and could afford to lose this battle and many more. One mistake on their part, however, and the entire HLF movement was done for.

CHAPTER 22

After the successful mission, the HLF took a week off to refit, regroup, and sleep. After everyone was well rested and well fed, Austin and Steve put out the word that there would be a briefing about the next mission coming soon, and that everyone needed to go through their gear again and make sure that everything was battle ready. There were moans and groans from the HLF soldiers, and it made John wonder if he was fighting alongside soldiers or grade school youth scouters.

Before the briefing began, Austin surveyed the room. He looked around to see each person as an individual and made sure that they all knew that he was speaking to them personally, as well as to the group.

"Our last mission was a great success. We took the fight to them, and we won. While it will take some skill and a lot of luck, I think that we should follow that up with a raid on their biggest human slaughterhouse, HAPPY TIMES."

Loud whispers of amazement, some positive and some negative, went around the room. When people had started to settle down Austin continued:

"They won't be expecting it, and we will have surprise on our side. First, they won't be expecting us to strike so hard right in their main human slaughterhouse. Second, they won't be expecting us to hit them again so quick after we just attacked. If we can pull this off, we can turn the tide on this thing. We also figured out how to break into their TV system and we will film the horrors of that place and broadcast them later during one of the state organized cooking shows. If that isn't power to the people, I don't know what is."

Austin continued that he had a plan and produced an elaborate to- scale model of the slaughterhouse to illustrate its execution to the whole group. Tomorrow, at zero dark thirty, they would strike. The 30 of them would travel by night on foot to the perimeter of the Happy Times Slaughterhouse. Twenty-six of them would make up the assault team, and 2 teams of 2 would wait outside to stand guard in both the front and back. Unlike the previous missions, they would have walkie-talkies and be able to communicate with all the different elements as the plan unfolded.

Using silenced weapons, they would eliminate the gate

guards and the roving guard and move to surround the target. After obtaining the key cards from the dead guards, they would simultaneously enter the slaughterhouse by both the front and the rear doors. They would operate in teams of 4, clearing the slaughterhouse of all guards and SS forces before attempting to rescue any of the prisoners. All HLF fighters would be using silenced weapons only until they were detected. After that stealth goes out the window because it would be World War Three in there.

"Remember the 3 Ss for a successful mission," said Steve. "Speed, stealth, and savagery. We are going to strike them so hard and so fast and so awful that they have no idea what is coming until it's too late. We will rely on our former military brothers and sisters to lead each of the 6 assault teams. John, Austin, and Mary, you will be team leaders for your people. Martha, Devone, and I will lead our forces."

"Three teams will enter the front, and three teams will go in the back. Taking care NOT to shoot each other," he paused for emphasis and a few chuckles, "we will make our way to the middle. When we have eliminated all threats, we will cut the shackles off all the prisoners, set explosives, and retreat to a tunnel system in the mountains. Sadie and Pat will film the awful things happening to people in there so we can expose the cruelty for all to see."

He concluded, "Make no mistake. We will be in a fight for our lives in there. The SS Troopers and guards in there have been specially selected for their cruelty. They literally have to eat a baby alive to get that assignment."

The group stirred. That was a whole new level of fucked up. They had heard of these people doing bad things, but never this awful.

"It's true. Anyone who wears the death's head skull insignia on their uniform has had to do unspeakable things. As a result, they are well paid, well fed, and well trained. These guys are fanatics and will crawl over broken glass just to have a chance to kill you and eat you and your family alive. This is a fight to the death. They won't be taking prisoners, and neither will we. Flush feelings of pity, remorse, and compassion out of your headgear. We are there to save the prisoners and to KILL their captors. All of them. Any questions?"

Steve went over and over the plan again and again, until everyone knew what they were doing and could recite the plan forwards and backwards. The team leaders then went over their individual parts with their teams, making sure everyone was comfortable with what they were doing. John went through his team one by one and made sure that all of their gear was squared away, and that everyone got enough food and had a place to sleep.

As John did before every mission, he laid out all his gear and made sure all his weapons were cleaned, in good working order, and had easily accessible ammunition. He looked over his gear: battle sword, battle knife, submachine gun with silencer and 5 magazines, battle rifle with 7X scope and 3 magazines, blaster pistol and 2 magazines, and his 9mm pistol and 3 magazines. He then inspected his assault vest and his ammunition. He had a combined 254 bullets in mixed ammunition, enough for most combat missions. He felt good about that. Most of the members of the teams would be carrying far less, only the submachine gun and 5 magazines, which would mean that they would be able to move fast but wouldn't be able to dig in and fight for a prolonged period.

That night everyone stayed up late. The group talked and laughed nervously, knowing it might be their last night on earth. One of the Lincoln HLF had scrounged a card game called Tres and after learning how to play, they all sat around enjoying it and each other's company.

John and Joy waited until almost everyone had fallen asleep and then snuck into the ammunition room. Without saying a word, Joy locked the ammo room door and John put a Woobie blanket on the ground. While they were indoors, the setting was less than ideal, and the floor was hard and cold.

They stood there in the middle of that lonely room, surrounded by guns, bullets and grenades. Once they had neatly undressed, their eyes locked on each other. They embraced and his lips found hers.

They fornicated like ninjas, not making a sound so they didn't wake the sleeping rest of the HLF. There was a quiet desperation to the act of love making. This could very well be their last night on earth, and if it wasn't, well, that day was coming soon enough.

John and Joy stared into each other's eyes, and John

smiled. Yes, he was scared as hell, but he couldn't help but smile. Though he had never said the words aloud, he loved her. She was his heaven locked inside this hell.

They lay there in each other's arms, wrapped in the blanket for warmth. John wished with all insanity the dawn's light would never come. They promised each other that they would stay awake and talk, but the warmth of Joy's embrace lured John to sleep. He closed his eyes for only a moment, and when he opened them, the sun in his eyes told him the new day had arrived.

CHAPTER 23

The group left in the middle of the night. They kept in the shadows, traversing the town like urban ninjas. They moved quietly and deliberately, scanning the horizons for possible targets and threats. After about an hour of very slow travel, they reached the front gate of the Happy Times Slaughterhouse. Without talking, John, Steve, and Austin low crawled over to the gate. They watched for about 5 minutes until they were certain that only two guards were present. In unison, Steve and Austin popped up and shot the guards, while John stood lookout.

Steve and Austin were just about to give the all- clear signal when the roving guard showed up. It took a second for the guard to realize what was happening, and when he did, it was too late. John shot him twice with his silenced 9 mm pistol and then went over to the twitching body to put a third into the guard's face as he lay dying on the ground. Everyone froze and listened to hear if they had been discovered. No sounds. So far, their luck was holding.

As they had planned, the assault teams moved into

position and the HLF sentries maneuvered themselves outside, two in the front and two in the back. They took the keycards from the guards and gave one to each team. When everyone was ready and in place, Steve said the code words over the walkie-talkies.

"Green Hell!"

The front and back assault teams simultaneously opened the doors with their key cards and filed inside. They knew that they were about to see some crazy shit, but somehow this place exceeded their expectations.

The Happy Times Slaughterhouse was an industrial assembly line of murder. There were pens for keeping prisoners and a stockade for holding a person while he was about to be processed into dead meat. First, the person was decapitated. Then his arms and legs were cut off. Finally, the torso was split in two. The pieces were separated into piles of heads in one area, piles of torsos in another, and lastly, piles of limbs. The "usable' meat was cleaved from the limbs and torsos then thrown onto a conveyer belt, which slowly rolled towards a processing area. The floor was covered in blood that dripped from the limbs. Not much care was put into keeping anything clean. The stench of death was overwhelming.

Hundreds of prisoners were in the pens at any given time, and the noise from yelling, screaming, and crying was deafening. The whole sight was nauseating and quite disturbing, but John was concentrating on the mission. He thanked their luck for the noise, for it would muffle the sound of their gunshots. His team advanced. They scanned for danger as they moved through the aisles.

The first guard saw them and went to unsling his rifle, but Joy dropped him with a shot. John turned and zipped 3 shots into another guard, and then another. They walked in a semi-crouching position, moving and shooting as one. Up until this point, they hadn't met with any real resistance and were moving quite quickly through the slaughterhouse.

They turned a corner and John and Joy exchanged a brief smile. Suddenly, Joy's head exploded into blood, and life left her eyes. Joy had been shot. John stared for a moment, his brain not wanting to comprehend what he was seeing. He ran to her, but there was nothing he could do but embrace her corpse as she whimpered a final goodbye. She was gone. John looked down at his bloody hands. His mind flashed to his time with Joy. He wanted to go into a hysterical panic, to just sit down and give up, but through an incredible act of self-control and discipline, he cast off those thoughts and got up.

"Fuck it," John mumbled and spat. For some reason, spitting his contempt always made him feel better.

John looked up and saw the SS Trooper responsible. The Trooper turned to fire at John, but John dropped a burst of submachine gun fire into the general area the SS Trooper was in. The SS Trooper ducked, then wildly returned fire back at John. John changed magazines while the remaining members of his team fired at the Trooper. John turned to tell them to get down, but just as he turned, one of them got his face blown off. The other HLF soldier hugged the ground like it was his mother, a hard lesson learned.

It was clear to John the Trooper's vest was absorbing most of the shots. He dropped the submachine gun on the ground, along with his remaining magazines, and unslung the heavy battle rifle, bringing it up to his shoulder. When the

Trooper came into his scope, he sent a single shot flying and the Trooper's head disappeared into red mist. John blessed the high caliber bullets in the rifle and their damage capabilities but realized that he would have to be stingy with his shots due to his limited amount of ammunition.

John and his remaining teammates scanned for threats as they moved slowly along the aisles. The shots from the SS Trooper had alerted his comrades and everyone else in the slaughterhouse that they were under attack. There wasn't any need for stealth anymore, just quick violence towards any threats. A gunshot caused John to quickly turn his rifle in the direction of three Troopers. Their shots went wild, but John's didn't. He gunned down the middle guy first and was leveling onto his next target when his teammate dropped a full magazine of 9mm into the other two Troopers' faces. Seeing their targets were eliminated, they moved on.

John wasn't sure how the other members of the assault teams were fairing, but he didn't like what he had seen so far. Less than 10 minutes into the mission and his squad was down by 50%, all KIA. He didn't like those statistics. He gritted his teeth and moved on, putting a burst of rifle fire into a guard and a Trooper who were moving towards them. His teammate shot another guard then fell to the ground after being shot in the arm. John whirled and emptied the rest of his magazine into that Trooper.

Cursing his heavy trigger finger, John dropped the empty magazine and locked a fresh one into his rifle. The gun made a satisfying "chunk" sound when John sent the bolt forward. The weapon was ready to fire once again, and not a minute too soon. An SS Trooper stepped forward and almost got off a shot towards them, but John took off his face with two shots.

John reached down, grabbed his teammate, and moved forward. He had the battle rifle in one hand and her in the other. They continued to shuffle forward, purposefully blocking out the gunfire, screams, and chaos all around them to focus only on THE MISSION. John felt a burning pain and then looked down. A bullet had sliced through his arm and into his teammate's head. She was dead. He dropped her lifeless body and turned towards the direction the shot had come from. Shots roared from his rifle, killing a guard, a Trooper, and a piece of machinery behind them.

He moved forward shooting, taking out guards here and there, only stopping to change magazines.

John locked the last magazine into place and with a grunt of pain, moved forward. He could see blood trickling down his arm and was glad that it was just a trickle and not a spurt. He shot to the left and to the right, and with a final rat- tat- tat, the last magazine was empty. He dropped the rifle and pulled out his SD Megablaster pistol.

John's walkie-talkie squawked to life. "This is the rear guard. We have company." And then, "Front guard here. We are surrounded! We will fight it out but be advised that when they are done with us, they are going to come for you. Good luck!" The walkie-talkie squawked again, but this time, it was only sounds of gunfire. No more voices.

"FUCK," said John, to no one in particular. He looked off into space, as if momentarily lost in a dream. Flashes of better days, and pictures of his family and friends danced in his brain. Then the situation came back into focus. John snapped out of it just in time to see a Trooper raising his rifle up towards him. Almost in slow motion, John pulled the trigger and watched a mess of death vomit out of the blaster, as if he had grabbed a dragon by the tail and made it burp fire. The recoil was painful and the gunshot deafening, but the Trooper was dead, and John was alive.

John shot another SS Trooper, then another guard, then another Trooper. He reached the holding pen for the prisoners, shot another two guards, and then shot the lock off the door. The naked prisoners ran out and started attacking guards and the SS, taking weapons from the dead and attempting to shoot their way out. The blaster pistol roared to life again, claiming the life of another guard, then another, until he was down to his last magazine.

John saw Austin across the way and met up with him. He was limping, presumably from a gunshot. They exchanged a glance that said, "we are really fucked now," before looking out the window. They were indeed surrounded. There were about two hundred fully armed SS Troopers outside, with helicopters and tanks.

"Well, now what?" asked John.

"Looks like we are going to have to shoot it out," said

Austin.

"Shit,' said John.

"Don't let yourself be captured," said Austin. "They will torture you and your family and most likely eat you alive."

"Ok, so what's the bad news?" quipped John.

The building shook and John looked over to see that the culprit was a tank rumbling through the front door. John shot the first two Troopers who tried to follow the tank in, and then jumped up onto the tank. As luck would have it, the top hatch of the tank was open. John popped the lid and shot his blaster pistol dry, killing the tank crew. He then threw his explosives in the tank, closed the hatch, and ran like hell. The tank's armored shell gave the small explosives the effect of a pressure cooker. The shrapnel from the exploding tank killed ten advancing Troopers and wounded countless others.

It was a desperate last stand. The SS Troopers poured in from all sides. John was down to his 9mm pistol, moving and shooting and trying to make every shot count. He quickly burned through all the ammo and before long, he was out of that too. He unsheathed the battle sword and turned it on. The sword vibrated malevolently in his hand, almost begging John to allow it to drink blood.

"LET'S DANCE, MOTHERFUCKERS!" roared John, as he charged a pack of oncoming SS Troopers.

John took off the first man's head, cut the second one in half, and put his sword through the third. He was about to try for a fourth when he was hit from behind. John stumbled to his knees, dropping the sword. He pulled out the battle knife and swiped at the set of feet in front of him, severing a foot and toppling the howling Trooper. John tried to get to his feet again when he was knocked back on the ground. The last thing he saw before the darkness engulfed him was Steve being shot in the head by a grinning Commander.

CHAPTER 24

John gradually regained consciousness. As the world slowly came into a hazy focus, he realized that he was being beaten and tortured. Given the day's events, that seemed reasonable to him. He looked down and realized that his bullet wounds had been bandaged. The SS had patched him up only to beat him to death. Oh, the irony!

"Where are the rest of the hideouts? Give us names and locations if you want your family to live! Help us and you will be spared!"

John opened his eyes and stared at his attacker. "Come closer and I'll tell you."

The man came closer. "Closer," John whispered. "Closer," he whispered again. The man moved closer to John. "Let me whisper it in your ear."

The man put his ear in John's face and John bit it right off. The man screamed in pain and John spit the man's ear back in the man's face. Guards rushed in to help the screaming man.

"Would you fucking pussies hurry up and fucking kill me

already? Jesus H Fucking Christmas, what do I have to do for a death sentence around this turd castle? Hey you- yeah you, dickless- I fucked your mom and your sister the other day while your dad watched. I think the prick actually enjoyed watching what a real vegan man can do."

The guard flushed red with rage and unslung his rifle.

"Yes, oh yes, your mom LOVED it! Not so much your sister though. She only likes to get banged in the ass, and that's not my thing."

John was cracked in the mouth before he could continue his tirade. He spit blood in the guard's face and let out a howl of a laugh.

"HA-HA-HA! I have HIV 20, Hep X, Covid 40 and it's all fucking yours, you fucking fuck. You would kill me already if you had any balls, you fucking limp dick fuck!"

John went on to curse all their mothers, fathers, sisters, brothers, grandparents, and extended kin. He called them every insult in the book and then created some right there on the fly. John was scared to die, but now the thought of what might happen to his family if he lived was far more terrifying.

"Everyone, everyone, would you all please calm down. We have a guest. Let's make him feel at home, and welcome. Why are you beating this poor boy?"

The beatings stopped and everyone quieted down, turning to look and see who was talking. The Commander entered the cell, grinning ear to ear and carrying a tablet. He looked down at the tablet and then over at John.

'Savage, John D. Born July 4, 2020, son to Robert and Maria Savage…."

The Commander paused and looked up from the tablet.

"Johnny Fucking Savage?! What kind of fucking name is that? And you were born on the Fourth of July? What are you, an action hero from the 1980's?"

John looked over at the Commander and smiled, blood dripping from his mouth.

"Maybe I am," John said, in a low voice.

After a good chuckle at his own joke, the Commander continued reading out loud.

"Normal childhood, some sports – football, wrestling and track? Joined the Army at twenty years of age as a paratrooper, went on to be a US ARMY RANGER. Two tours of duty later, a WAR HERO, and look at you now. One big fucking mess."

The Commander continued. "You've given my guys quite a run for their money. I applaud you for that. How many Troopers did you kill today? And now, poor Gilbert here will have a hard time listening to his music in stereo, and he loves that, you know. Good work with that, too. You really are a special boy and deserve extra special treatment."

The Commander broke into song. "Don't worry about a thing. Because everything is going to be alright."

The Commander smiled, showing his pearly whites. "I'll tell you what. We are both grown-ups, so I won't bullshit you. No fairytales with happy endings HA-HA-HA. I plan on killing you and there is nothing that you can do to change that. I am a man of my word, though. You tell us what we want to know right now, and I won't eat your family in front of you on live TV. You tell me what I want to know, and I will shoot you right here and all the suffering ends."

John swallowed his fear. "I used to think you were super

scary. Now I know you are just a creepy old man that likes to scare people and fuck little boys, so you can go fuck yourself too. If you were a man, you would kill me right now. All of this tough talk is boring the shit out of me."

John smiled a little bit on the inside. That sounded a lot like something one of his favorite action heroes of his youth might have said in a similar situation. At least he could die knowing that he didn't go out like some punk.

The Commander smiled. "Thank you for that. The President told me that I had to put information as the priority, over the pleasure of killing and eating you and your family. Since there is no deal to be made, I get to have my fun. In the end, you are going to wish you had told us what we wanted to know."

He turned to the guards.

"Put him on suicide watch."

CHAPTER 25

Holden was at a crossroads. He had been forced to do so many awful things and couldn't see any reasonable path to regain his humanity and redeem himself. For months, he had dulled those thoughts with drugs and alcohol, and had to take sedatives to keep the nightmares away. He had become the devil himself just to stay alive, living only for the hope of REVENGE.

Sometimes, after a night of drinking and fucking, he had put his blaster pistol in his mouth, contemplating ending it all, and going to sweet oblivion. There were only two things that stopped him from taking his own life. The first was his belief in God. He knew that if there was a God, he would surely end up in hell because of what he had done.

The second was revenge. All the things that he had done to stay alive had been because of the Commander. He reasoned that if he could make the SS trust him, then maybe, just maybe, he would have a shot at redemption. Maybe put a shot into the Commander's head while he was at it.

When Holden heard about the showdown with the HLF

and the capture of his former classmate, Gloria's brother, he started to think of how this could fit into his plan for revenge. Obviously, John would have a motive to help him kill the Commander, but because of who and what Holden had become, there was a possibility that John would kill him as well. Holden reasoned this would be an acceptable risk and decided that it would be ok if he died. Good riddance to bad rubbish, as one of his teachers used to say. He would just have to come up with a way to talk to John, tell him who he is and what he had planned.

Holden heard from fellow Troopers that John was on an around the clock suicide watch. Because John was a priority prisoner, he would have to have two Troopers always guarding him. The need to have two Troopers stand guard constantly meant that all the lower ranking Troopers were enlisted into this duty. As luck would have it, Holden was also placed on the guard duty rotation. He waited for an opportunity to talk to John alone, biding his time.

The first shift saw no such chance, as the other guard didn't ever get tired or need a bathroom break. That Trooper, Richard, was older and by the book. Holden took every opportunity to call him "Dick" because, well, the guy was a major dick.

The second shift was different. The guard he was paired with this time was a lazy drunk. Holden took the chance to talk to John when the guard went to the bathroom to relieve himself.

Holden came close to the bars. He looked both ways and whispered into the cell. "PSST. John. Hey John. You awake?"

John's response was to be expected.

"Go fuck yourself."

Holden, undaunted, continued, "I knew your sister. I was at the rally where she was captured."

John stirred in his cell. "And?"

Holden, encouraged by the reaction, told him the story of how he became a part of the SS, from the beginning up to the present. He told the story in pieces, as quickly as he could while the other guard was on bathroom breaks. He didn't omit any of the awful details and gave it as raw as it was.

John laid back down on his hard cell bunk. "That's some really fucked up shit. So, why tell me? I'm sure you could guess all the bad things I would do to a turd like you if I got out of here. I would probably kill you harder than I would one of these other assholes. So why bother telling me?"

Holden laid it all on the line. Revenge, plain and simple. Holden was no longer happy with the deal he made with the devil- his soul in exchange for his life. He had been forced into becoming part of the evil system that had killed John's sister and murdered millions of others. He had come to realize the one thing that he wanted more than being alive was revenge, but he needed John's help. Holden wanted to die; he just didn't want to die for nothing.

John looked at Holden. "I'll think about it."

Holden said, "Ok, well think fast, they are ramping up for you and your family's execution."

John smiled. "Ok fuck it then, let's do it."

Holden made one condition: he was to be the one that killed the Commander. John chuckled. "Alright hero, shit, he's yours. What do you have in mind?"

When Holden was finished talking, John contemplated the plan. A day of reckoning was coming, and every one of these SS fuckers had an appointment with death.

CHAPTER 26

Earlier in the week, the SS announced John and his family would be guests on the popular TV show *What's Cooking Good Looking?* On the show, Hollywood celebrities tasted body parts cooked from the unfortunate "guests", who were often prisoners of the state. The objective was for them to guess which part of the guest's body the meal came from. At the end of the show, all the audience members were awarded cash prizes, and some were selected at random to take part in the executions. It was a fan favorite when they got children to do the killing. Sometimes they even raped one of the women -or men- on live TV.

The government considered the show a win-win. Not only was the government able to publicly dispose of their political enemies, but they were also able to get the buy-in from the public. The popularity of the show condoned their acts of violence. The state- run churches said they were doing the "work of the Lord", and that it was a sin to not watch, because God himself had promised them "meat." The show helped to desensitize people to violence and normalize the government sanctioned murders.

John was led onto the stage in chains by an entourage of political and Hollywood elite. There were senators, directors, stars and starlets, and even a few of John's heroes from when he was a kid. Looking around, John would have been star- struck if the situation had been different. John joked with the celebrities and asked a starlet for her autograph. Of course, the crowd thought it was hilarious that John could joke and laugh when he was about to be brutally murdered. Even John himself chuckled at how truly grim the situation was. "Fuck, life certainly does suck sometimes," he thought.

John's parents were already in position, alive and awake but with tourniquets placed on all four limbs so they wouldn't die immediately when they were carved up. They also had gags on their mouths so they couldn't scream and interrupt everyone's fun. John was placed in an electric chair styled apparatus, with electronic four-point restraints built into the chair. He was sickened by what these assholes planned to do to his parents. He was reminded once again about how the barbaric treatment of his family mirrored how society used to treat animals before they were all extinct. He tried to put his feelings out of his mind, slow his breathing, and focus on the plan.

The "plan," if one could call it that, was that at a prearranged point in the show, Holden would press the remote release button for John's restraints, leaving John free to take a gun from one of the guards. Holden would be backstage with a sniper rifle making sure that John was able to free his parents and execute the politicians. Holden would then shoot the Commander. The plan ended there. They would keep fighting until they were dead, or they had won. Neither of them thought escape was likely, but if they did, they would meet up at a safe house and decide the next step from there.

The lights dimmed. There was a hushed silence, then the theme song began. The show's host, Guy Smiley, came running out from behind the curtain. The audience applauded loudly This was indeed a popular show.

"Good evening, ladies and germs, and welcome to our show…can you say it with me?"

As one, the host and the audience said, "What's Cooking Good Looking!" There was much applause.

"That's right, thank you very much for that! We have a great show for you tonight, boy do we ever! Tonight, we will be roasting and barbequing enemy of the state and HLF enforcer Johnny Savage, his father Rob, and his mother Maria."

After another round of applause the celebrity guests were introduced, and they got to joke around with the audience. One of the well–known guests was Chef Jenkins, who declared that he could tell the way that someone was going to taste just by looking at them. His tag line was, "I skipped lunch, so I'm having seconds." When the chef said his catch phrase this time, you could almost make out what John was muttering through his teeth. If the camera had zoomed in on John, one would have seen him glaring at Chef Jenkins and saying,

"I'm going to feed you your own tongue, you fucking fuck."

After some more jokes and a demented spin of the wheel, the time had come for the butcher to sheer some flesh from both parents. Two men in butcher outfits came out on stage, took a bow to the audience, and approached John's mom and dad. There was a showy bit with them sharpening their knives, and then they took another bow.

Just as they were about to carve up their victims, the first and then the second butcher stopped in their tracks and suddenly fell to the ground. The audience, along with the rest of the TV crew and the SS, didn't know what was going on. Was this part of the act, all in fun, or was this really happening? No one could tell, and the crowd went silent. In that space of time John's feet and hand restraints opened. He was FREE!

CHAPTER 27

John turned to face the SS Troopers that were standing behind him. Unfortunately for them, while John was a trained fighter with countless knockouts to his name, these men were chosen for this assignment based on their good looks. The first Trooper was so surprised that he didn't even raise his hands to defend himself. John's first punch broke the man's nose, his second, the man's jaw, and his third put the Trooper on the ground for good.

John walked over to the downed Trooper's unconscious body and lifted his right leg. With all his might, John stomped down on the Trooper's skull. The man's head instantly broke apart like a watermelon being smashed with a sledgehammer. John got brains and cerebral spinal fluid all over his shoes. He left a trail of bloody footprints behind him as he casually walked towards the next Trooper.

This Trooper wasn't going down without a fight. He threw a punch which John easily blocked. Then he landed a punch, winding John for a moment. John smiled at the man and then kicked him in the shin with all his might. He broke the Trooper's leg, exposing the man's tibia and sending blood everywhere. The Trooper let out a howl. John leaned back and sent a combo of punches into action. The first two punches landed, and the third put the man on the ground. John picked up the wounded Trooper's blaster pistol, pulled the side back and shot the man in the head at point-blank range, blowing the man's head clear off his shoulders.

John shot the remaining Troopers and guards that were still on stage with him. After emptying his blaster pistol, he picked a battle rifle off the floor and sent a full magazine of bullets whizzing wildly into the audience, indiscriminately killing and wounding dozens of celebrities and politicians. He changed magazines and turned towards a surprised Commander. He placed the man in his sights and smiled.

The Commander was stunned, paralyzed by what he was seeing and unable to comprehend this reversal of fortune. How was this man not dead?!

John decided that a bullet was too good for the Commander. He took a razor-sharp butcher knife from the corpse of the closest dead chef and cut the Commander from his navel to his sternum with a single slash.

John watched as the dying man lay drowning in his own blood. The Commander tried in vain to remake his belly, struggling to put the protruding organs and intestines back where they belonged. John watched him scramble and slosh around for a few moments and then stepped forward to finish the job with the blaster rifle. He put the rifle's crosshairs on the Commander's head and went to pull the trigger, but Holden's bullet found the Commander first. John looked up. He saw someone wave, who he presumed was Holden. "Cheeky bastard," he thought.

It was satisfying to see the skull fragments and cavitated face of this evil man. John took one last look and stomped down on the Commander's head. It was incredible to John how scary this man had been just mere hours ago, but in the blink of an eye the man had quickly folded. Now John was smashing this man's skull and literally dancing on his grave. "Payback is such a motherfucker," thought John.

He freed his parents then handed his dad a blaster pistol and his surprised mom a 9mm pistol. The three of them moved to the exit, shooting at everyone in front of them. His parents were registered pacifists, but after almost being eaten alive, they were a little less inclined to show mercy or turn the other cheek towards their enemies.

Upon exiting the television studio, Holden's explosive charges went off, killing everyone left inside. John thought about the day's turn of events. Those people had come to feast on him and his parents, but instead, had been burned alive, becoming BBQ themselves. John and his parents fled to the safe house Holden had told him about, yet again traveling through the sewers.

It would have been a joyful reunion, but the shadow of Gloria's death and their probable capture loomed over them. John told his parents everything that had happened since he left in the botched rescue of his sister. The safe house had a kitchen and they were able to have a meal as a family once more. John wanted to cry, but he held it in because he didn't see the point to the tears. After the traumatic events of the day, he didn't want to stress his parents out even more.

Hours later Holden showed up, arms full of guns and

ammunition, along with another SS Trooper. John almost shot

him, but the Trooper took off his helmet and mask.

"Austin! What in the actual fuck?! How did you escape?"

"I didn't. I was arrested and tortured, just like you. I

thought I was a goner for sure, then Holden found me and told

me he wanted my help for some revenge plot and then I was sure

that I was dead. I helped with your getaway at the TV studio."

Holden told John's parents the whole story, of how he

had known Gloria, and of all the unspeakable things he had done

just to stay alive. John's parents remembered Holden, as he had

briefly dated Gloria in high school.

"Hmm," thought John, "the plot thickens. Could this be

some sort of unrequited love motivation?"

That night, after John's parents had gone to sleep,

Holden revealed the plan. They would give John's parents a map

through the sewers to a permanent safe house in the countryside,

along with food and water, flashlights, and everything they would

need for survival.

They would then tell John's parents that they are splitting

up because they are wanted fugitives, and that they would meet up again later. They would give his parents new identities and a way to contact the HLF out there for food and water in the meantime.

They themselves would not be going into hiding though. The three of them would be going for one final strike to the evil heart of the system that had caused so much death, so much destruction, and so many tears. They would be going to the one place where no one would be expecting them to go. Instead of running and hiding, they would be going right for the jugular. They would assault the Presidential Palace. It was a foolhardy plan with almost no chance of success, but because it was so ludicrous, neither the SS nor the government would be expecting it.

While it was a suicide mission, they did also have an ace hidden up their sleeves. The SS had been experimenting with special suits to make their Troopers into super soldiers. The suits were bulletproof, had an internal air filtering system so they were impervious to tear gas, and were fireproof. The built-in robotic processors had a GPS and navigation system, which would show the wearer the number of people moving in the area, allowing them to determine the number of threats. Best of all, the suits had a built-in exoskeleton, giving the wearer boosted strength and the ability to punch through concrete walls, bend steel, and other such abilities usually limited to comic book superheroes. They had the force of a medium-sized car moving at full speed and were rated to endure the impact of the same magnitude. There were only three known working prototypes and they were going to steal them all.

John shook his head in amazement at the plan and laughed. "Y'all fucking crazy, but at least you have balls. Ok, fuck it, I'm in. Let's go get that pink motherfucker!"

Later that day, John said a painful goodbye to his parents. It was especially hard because he had to pretend he would see them again and that their separation was only temporary. Lying to his folks always bothered John, but he knew the truth would only hurt them in this case. When they left, he felt relieved. Not because he wanted them to go, but because at least then he wouldn't have to keep lying to them. That shit was a lot of work.

CHAPTER 28

Austin, Holden, and John arrived at the Special Services compound just after midnight. The office buildings always looked creepy, but the complex was particularly ominous at night. Spotlights illuminated the gigantic stone eagle on the front of the building and the banner that hung above the front entrance. John stopped and looked up to read the banner. "The Department of SPECIAL SERVICES: Working together towards a better future for all Americans." John smirked at the bullshit of it all.

While the Special Services were on high alert, the three passed easily through the first security checkpoint. Holden had brought an extra SS uniform for John, and he had forged keycards and identification credentials for all three of them. They did their best to look like they knew where they were going and what they were doing. Holden had coached Austin and John the night before.

"Look, it's all about acting," Holden had said. "And acting is all about believing in the role. In this situation, your role is one of SS Officers. We are on official business to transfer these

MK Ultra suits so that the terrorists don't get their hands on them. You have to BELIEVE that to be the truth, or everything falls apart."

John had said his cover name, "Steven Powers," and his date of birth and identification number so many times that night, chanting them almost as if in yogic meditation. He had tried to conjure up a life story for this guy. Maybe Steven had been in the military as he had, perhaps the same unit. Maybe he had deployed to the same place. Maybe he had gone to the same schools. Pretty soon, the character named "Steven Powers" had become a real, believable person, flesh and blood.

They would all be wearing helmets and would blend right into the scenery. In the case they had to remove their helmets, Holden had decided that Austin and himself would probably not be recognized. John on the other hand, was a different story. His face was all over the TV box, and soon there would be "WANTED" posters hanging in every town square in America. Holden's way around that – cheap props.

Holden applied makeup to John's face, which covered some of his bruises. John also sported a fake mustache that looked ridiculous, yet was in fashion among many in the SS. They dyed John's hair and added an eye patch. The result was a cover that would probably hold up, if no one made any mistakes. While Holden and Austin seemed very optimistic about the plan, John thought otherwise. Things never went the way they were planned, and you just had to roll with it.

They were questioned a final time at the last checkpoint. Unlike the other checkpoints, however, this time they were told to remove their helmets and state their names and identification numbers. They all did as they were told. John made sure to think positive thoughts as he did so, believing the lie.

"Man, you look like you've been through the ringer," remarked the Trooper as he looked at John's fake credentials.

"Well, you should see the other guy," said John with a laugh in the voice of "Steven Powers."

John went on. "Those fucking HLF rebels really fucked things up at Happy Times. One of my friends was shot, and I got clobbered pretty good when a tank exploded."

The Trooper looked one last time at John's ID card, then handed it back to him.

"Yeah, I was there that day. That rebel scum killed one of my friends too. I wish I had five minutes alone with that piece of shit Johnny Savage. I would kill him, gut him, and serve him to President White on a silver platter myself."

John smiled, playing along, while thinking how weird it was to recall the recent shootout at the Happy Times Slaughterhouse, but from the SS perspective.

Holden hesitated. Were they recognized? Should they start shooting? Holden considered the odds. They were only armed with blaster pistols, and they were outnumbered at least a thousand to three. Once they started shooting there would be no chance of survival. However, this motherfucker right here would be dead. What was it going to be?

The Trooper gave them back their passes and waved them through. Austin and Holden said a few quick words of thanks. John thanked the Trooper for his service. When they were well past the guards, they all took a huge sigh of relief.

They walked down a long corridor and took some twists and turns, and soon they were in the laboratory area. As they were approaching the part of the labs that housed the suits they had come for, they passed a door marked "EXPERIMENTS." Austin and Holden kept walking, but John stopped. Austin was about to give John a talking to and tell him to stick to the plan, but John had already opened the door and went inside. Austin told Holden, and the two of them went inside as well.

What they saw in the labs was shocking, even considering the brutality and terror they had witnessed first-hand at the Dairy Farm and at Happy Times Slaughterhouse. In one area, twins were surgically conjoined at the face. A "scientist" was monitoring the brain activity of each twin. When they would stab one of the twins with a rusty knife, the other twin would cry out in pain, and the brain activity of the other twin would go up. The scientist who was recording these findings kept saying, "Amazing," to himself.

"Yeah, amazingly cruel," John muttered under his breath. Luckily, only Austin heard him, and they quickly moved on.

In another area, children were locked into chairs and their eyes were forced open by a vice that went around the children's faces. "Scientists" were spraying chemicals into the children's eyes while other "scientists" were writing down their reactions on clipboards. Blood was flowing from the children's eyes, running down their little faces and onto the floor.

In yet another area, children sat in neat rows with their little arms in vices. One of the "scientists" flayed skin from their little arms, and the other one put drops of a chemical into the wounds. A third man wearing a lab coat was writing something on his clipboard every time a child had the acid dropped into their wounds.

A banging sound got their attention and they looked over in the direction of the noise. There was a machine that was testing how much force a human skull could take. John watched as one of the men set the machine to 50 PSI, and then pressed a big red button which sent a robotic arm holding a mallet crashing into a little girl's face. The girl dropped to the ground and her body was thrown into a gigantic bin labeled "garbage." Another child took her place, and the process was repeated.

Some of the children were crying, while others had just accepted their fate and were waiting for death in whimpering silence. John wanted to scream. He wanted to cry. He wanted to do something. He knew if he did, however, they would not be able to carry out their mission. While they might rescue one child, it would only be one, and that wasn't enough. They needed to save them all. With the most supreme self-control, John backed out of the room, and along with him, Holden and Austin.

Austin closed the door behind them. They passed a few other doors along the way and then they came to the end of the hall. The sign above the door read "SPECIAL SERVICES LABORATORY" in very official looking letters. Unlike many of the other doors, this one required a key card for entry. Austin and John paused to look at Holden, giving him a "Now what?" look that was not visible because they were wearing helmets. Holden produced a key card and held it up, much like a knight would have held up the holy grail. Holden swiped the card. The men held their breath, expecting a red light and to be denied entry but praying for a green light.

After a brief second, the green light came on. All three of them noted it, then looked at each other. They took a collective sigh of relief. Holden opened the door and they walked inside. No turning back now.

John was impressed by the size of the laboratory. There were stations for every type of weapon imaginable, from next generation blaster pistols to battle knives for testing. He stopped to look at some futuristic weapons called "laser guns." An SS Trooper in a jumpsuit held a gun-like object in both hands, and on the end of the weapon, was a power cord that was attached to a very heavy looking backpack.

The Trooper was smoking a state-issued cigarette and complaining to the technician on duty that the backpack was heavy and that he hated this "shit detail." The lab tech laughed. "Well, at least you aren't that guy," he said, pointing. "Count your blessings."

John followed the direction of the lab tech's pointing finger. About 50 feet down range was a prisoner hanging on the back wall by his wrists, his feet dangling in the air. The prisoner was wearing a white t- shirt with a bullseye printed on it. John thought to himself that it was ironic to have the prisoner confined in this position. After all, this was the international sign for "Don't shoot," and that's what they were about to do to this poor guy.

The Trooper lowered his protective goggles. He gave a thumbs up and switched his weapon on. A scary humming sound came from the backpack. After a minute of "warming up," a green light on the top of the backpack lit up. Seeing that, the lab tech gave a thumbs up, and the SS Trooper pulled the trigger.

An arc of lightening erupted from the nozzle of the "laser gun," and traveled in a slow zigzag toward its target. John watched in horror as the beam of light hit the prisoner in the chest.

"Bulls- eye!" yelled the Trooper.

The prisoner's torso exploded into a gooey, bloody mess. The man remained hanging from the chains, but his midsection was completely missing. John could hear some muffled cries coming from the prisoner. 'Damn that's fucked up," thought John.

The Trooper went for a second shot, but the weapon shorted and blew up in the Trooper's hands. Unfortunately, neither the Trooper nor the lab tech were harmed.

"Too bad," thought John. "They would have had it coming."

Holden came back for John, grabbing him by the arm.

"Time to go."

The men walked down the hall until they got to a final door marked MK ULTRA. Holden opened it and they entered. This part of the lab was more for storage and display than for experiments. Three MK ULTRA exoskeleton suits were on display in heroic looking poses in the middle of the room. On the left side of the room were some charging stations for battery packs. On the right side were weapons and accessories stored in neat rows.

Holden went behind the display and wheeled out a long cart. As one, they loaded the three suits onto the cart, along with the battery packs and a bunch of weapons. They stood back and looked at the equipment. It was stacked 6 feet. high.

"How the fuck are we not going to get caught?" asked John.

There was no answer to John's question. Holden made an "ok" circle gesture with his hand, and Austin said, "Let's go."

Holden was surprised at how easy it was to get the MK suits out of the lab. Part of it, he thought, was that they "looked" like they knew what they were doing. Only once was their pass checked, and that was when they were exiting the facility.

The rickety cart had a broken wheel, so wheeling the cart with the thousand plus pounds of equipment on it seemed to take forever. When they finally got to exit and their passes were checked a final time, they moved the cart into position, and Holden backed up a grey SS sprinter van for easy loading. They were done and sitting in the van in no time. Holden was in the driver's seat, Austin was riding shotgun, and John was in the rear with the gear.

Holden fired up the truck and they all looked at each other. "Ok," he said, exhaling. "No turning back now."

"Let's go get this motherfucker," said John.

"It's hard to not respect your enthusiasm," Austin said with a smile.

The three of them drove through the night. While they had to know there was no reasonable chance of success, there was a weird sense of optimism in the air. John thought it felt more like he was going on a road trip than on a suicide mission. And with that thought, he closed his eyes and fell asleep.

CHAPTER 29

They drove all day and through the night, stopping only once to refuel the van. Holden and Austin were able to get out and stretch and use the bathroom, but John on the other hand, had to hide in the back and piss in a bottle. His picture had been shown on every TV station since his escape from the game show the previous day. His entire escape had been broadcasted live in full 5XK. There was no denying that John was responsible for the deaths of numerous politicians and celebrities. He might not be famous, but he was certainly infamous. He was as good as dead if he got caught, or even recognized, and because of this, he rode in the back of the van, uncomfortably hidden under all the gear.

It was a sunny day and a scenic drive, but neither of the passengers in the front were in the mood for scenery. None of them were under any pretensions about how this was going to end. John was the least worried of them all. It wasn't that he wasn't scared, it was just he was so miserable being cramped in the back of the van that he just wanted to get it all over with.

The van finally pulled into the capital around 7 PM EST.

Traffic was thick, and it took an hour to navigate the crowded streets and make their way towards their destination. They came upon the first checkpoint and passed with flying colors. The Bronze checking their papers barely looked at their IDs before waving them through. The SS made everyone nervous, even the Bronze.

The second and the third checkpoints were the same. While they had been originally nervous about being caught, that feeling had been replaced with a confident, bored normalcy. Of course, they were in a van, of course they were driving through town, nothing to see here, and no known enemies of the state hidden in the back of the van. Of course, they weren't going to kill anyone, just out for a Sunday- Funday drive.

As they approached the final checkpoint, Holden thought of something.

"John, get in one of the suits and pull the other two suits on top of you. Those suits are super heavy, and when the guards search the car, they won't be able to move the suits and will only check to make sure that no one is in the first one."

John complied and quickly put the suit on. It was snug

but not uncomfortable. The suit kept its form well and protected him from the weight of the other suits. The military had taught him to deal with his fears, but he still hated to feel trapped, and the heavy suits lying on top of him made him feel claustrophobic like none other. Still, he knew if they were discovered the mission would be finished before it even got started. He closed his eyes and thought of better times.

Austin and Holden had seen THE PRESIDENTIAL PALACE on the television box, but it was even more amazing to behold in person. The Palace was surrounded by a 20- foot- high fence adorned with the bloody heads of political dissidents and other enemies of the state. Doing some quick math in his head, Austin figured there must be hundreds, if not thousands, of freshly severed heads on top of the fence. Austin told Holden about his calculations. Holden whistled and agreed that was a lot of heads and a lot of chopping. The moral argument of beheading aside, it just seemed like a lot of work. The stench from all those heads baking in the hot sun was overpowering, even from inside the van with the windows rolled up.

Austin wondered for a second why the place wasn't

swarming with flies, because surely all those heads would attract bugs. He then remembered there weren't any flies anymore. Even though it had been years since the last animals and insects died off, Austin thought he would never get used to their absence.

The Palace had a fierce glare emanating from it. During the second year of his reign, the President had ordered that every part of the Palace's exterior be covered with 24 carat gold plating. If the sun was out and one looked directly at it in certain angles, the glare was so bright that it would hurt the eyes. The cost of this project was estimated to be in the billions.

Holden and Austin stared in amazement at the rows of crucified victims lining the street to the Palace. Austin wondered to himself if there would ever be an end to this age of insanity.

John had fallen asleep. He was on a beach, lounging on a relaxing chair, sipping on a drink with a little umbrella in it, watching a wave lazily roll in. His girlfriend was sitting in a chair next to him, and was enjoying a magazine, or maybe a crime novel. He inhaled deeply and could almost smell the salt in the air and feel the ocean breeze on his face.

John was about to ask his girlfriend what she was

reading when he was awoken from his reverie with a jolt. His girlfriend and the beach were replaced with harsh reality. John frowned.

"We are here," Austin said. "We've made it through all the checkpoints and are in the Presidential Palace parking area."

Austin and Holden also donned their suits. In order to not draw attention to themselves, they changed in the back of the van. John moved forward in the vehicle to give them room, but it was still crowded with both Austin and Holden trying to change in such a cramped space. When they were all dressed, John asked the question on everyone's mind.

"So, what's the plan?"

Holden laid it all out for them.

"Ok, according to the news, the President is going to address the nation from the Oval Office tonight at 9PM EST. I think we should drive the van straight through the Flower Garden, crash through the Oval Office, and come out shooting. Our suits come with a GPS tracker that will allow us to find the President anywhere on earth within 5 feet. Can you see that map screen with turn-by-turn navigation just above your right eye?

That yellow blip is the President, and right now he is in the West Wing, leaving the Palm Room and walking towards the Oval Office."

John thought and said, "We should probably pop tear gas and nerve gas around us to limit the number of heroes that we have to kill."

Holden quickly agreed. "Good idea," he said, handing John a bunch of gas grenades.

John, Austin and Holden checked their gear and their weapons and said some prayers. Within 3 minutes, they were ready to go. They looked at each other. John gave a thumbs up and Austin nodded.

CHAPTER 30

Holden first drove at a relaxed, normal speed for a minute, then gunned the acceleration and veered towards the Flower Garden. They plowed through flowers, shrubbery, and a variety of outdoor items set up for a press conference event that was to happen tomorrow. Then the van hit a slightly elevated patch of earth which helped launch them towards the Presidential Palace walls.

The President was explaining to the American people that the economy was going to get better soon when he started to hear a faint rumble in the background. He tried to ignore it, but it got louder and louder. Suddenly, a van came crashing through the Office wall, splattering reporters and Secret Service Agents. The cameras quickly panned from the President to this van. What could possibly be going on?

The chaos and confusion left everyone stunned for a moment. Most people thought that this had been a terrible accident, and no one was moving. Then, above the momentary quiet, the screams came from one of the Secret Service Agents who had been mortally injured in the crash.

Holden was the first out of the vehicle. He didn't see the President, but from his GPS tracker he could tell he was very close. He leveled his battle rifle at the first threat and eliminated him, along with the Secret Service Agent right behind him. He also shot a couple of reporters, but that was more by accident than on purpose. Austin, still stunned from the collision, got out and joined the fight. He unslung his rifle and moved forward, looking for threats and targets.

John stumbled out of the van last. He had momentarily gotten tangled in some of the gear and had hit his head hard during the collision. He was seeing stars, but he knew that every minute counted in this race to get to the President.

"Now where is this pink motherfucker?" John muttered to himself as he awkwardly checked his GPS tracker. He could see the President was already out of the room, running down the hall towards the main building.

With maximum effort, John advanced through the room and out into the hall. He was hit with a bullet, which was followed by another and another. John could feel the bullets' impact, but they bounced harmlessly off the suit, with no more effect than being punched by a five-year-old.

Holden and Austin were already engaged in an all-out firefight with about twenty Secret Service Agents. They were winning but they were getting slowed down. John leveled his MG 42 machine gun and with a rat- a –tat- tat took out all twenty with a long burst of fire.

"More like killing a family of twenty," thought John.

John slung his MG 42 and took out a flamethrower and then proceeded to set both the Oval Office and the West Wing on fire, enjoying the warm glow.

The three of them slowly advanced. They were again stopped in the Palm Room by heavy weapons, but John set those men on fire, preferring to cook them versus shoot them. John watched the men burn to death with detached amusement and then looked at his GPS.

"It looks like the President is moving towards the East Wing," said John.

"Hmm he is probably going to the bunker in the East Wing. No worries. Let's head over there," said Holden.

The three of them sauntered towards the East Wing. A collection of Secret Service Agents and Troopers shot at them, but they were quickly dealt with. John smirked because it was straight out of his playbook when he was deployed, something he called "rake and bake." Rake the enemy with machine guns, then burn them with flamethrowers.

John turned the corner and a Trooper stepped behind him and shot John point-blank in the back of the head. John stumbled forward and then turned around. He looked the man in the eyes for a second and then punched him square in the face. The force of the blow was so powerful it separated the man's head from his body and launched it down the hall.

"Oh fuckkkk," laughed John, as he watched the head roll down the hall like a bloody soccer ball.

The GPS sure enough showed the President heading into the EMERGENCY OPERATIONS CENTER. They knew this would lock the President up tight and make it harder to get to him, which would make their job of ending his life harder. However, it would make it easier to end this chase, because once he was in the bunker, there would be no escape. They walked down the corridor until they were right above the bunker.

"What now?" asked John.

"I can tell you this - we aren't giving up," answered Austin.

"No one is suggesting that! Let's figure out how to get down to the entrance," said Austin.

They studied their GPS screens intently. After about 5 minutes, Holden excitedly announced he found a secret entrance way down towards the bunker. John and Austin followed close behind, knowing that every minute counted. They could tell they were getting somewhere when soldiers appeared in the stairwell and fired at them. They shot them dead and were about to go down the stairwell and into the bunker.

Something caught Holden's eye moving outside and he stopped for a second and looked out the window. The entire Department of Special Services had shown up! Thousands of SS Troopers, tanks, and helicopters had amassed outside. This was the same force that had invaded BOTH Canada AND Mexico, and now they were here for the three of them.

"There's no escape," he said.

They all stared outside for a minute, then John spoke.

"Who wants to escape? Let's get this pink motherfucker and finish the job we started. We'll deal with those fucks later."

Forty soldiers and Secret Service Agents later they reached the entrance to the bunker. There were so many dead bodies in such a tight space that John once again felt a little claustrophobic. He choked that fear back because he knew what was waiting for them, and it was much worse than his fear of tight spaces.

Holden pulled out some heavy-duty demolition cord, along with a bunch of explosives and crammed it all into a small space around the mechanism that closed and opened the door. He knew they didn't have enough to blow the door completely off its hinges, but to blow the lock off the door? Hmm, that was possible.

After they prepped the door, they stacked the dead bodies in front of it like cord wood to insulate themselves from the blast. They ran up the stairs and made sure the suits had the mute feature on so they didn't all go deaf.

They all looked at each other and nodded. Then, with a

mischievous smile Holden pressed a button on a transmitter that he was holding and the C-4 exploded. The explosion was deafening, but the three of them couldn't hear a thing. Finally, checking his watch, Holden suggested that they go take a look, and unmute their suits.

The explosion had turned the dead bodies into soup and had blown the door straight off its hinges. John and his companions entered the bunker and greeted the President and his entourage.

John spoke for them.

"Hi guys. It's been an emotional day for us all. We have come for the President, and while we are at it, the fucking vice president too. Anyone who wishes to live, such as friends, family, and cabinet members move over to your right. We will extend this courtesy to Secret Service Agents who drop their guns as well."

A Secret Service Agent leveled a rifle at John and shot him. John didn't even flinch, he just pulled out his blaster pistol and put a hole the size of a bowling ball right in the middle of the man's chest. He marveled that the man was able to remain standing for a good 5 seconds with half of his organs missing before collapsing on the floor.

The President shook an angry fist at them.. As he spoke, his pink toupee jiggled on his head.

"How dare you riff - raff come into my house! I AM THE PRESIDENT OF THE UNITED STATES OF AMERICA! I AM THE ONLY THING THAT KEEPS THIS COUNTRY FROM CHAOS! I AM THE BENEFACTOR OF ALL, THE PROVIDER OF MEAT!"

Holden stepped forward and turned on his helmet's live feed. What he saw through his visor would now be broadcast on TV stations all over America. He addressed the President and everyone in the room, along with the entire nation.

"You've hurt a lot of good people, President White. You've turned the country that I love upside down."

The President sneered.

"FUCK 'EM. If you want to make an omelet, then you are going to have to crack some eggs."

John was done talking. He leveled his flamethrower.

"Those who don't want to die here with the President best step aside."

There was a quick scramble of people distancing themselves from the President and the VP. Then John spoke in a low voice, the quiet before the storm.

"Y'all got any marshmallows?"

John let the firestorm rip. The President put up his arms to protect himself, as if there was a way that he could block the flames by flailing his arms. It was clear from their surprise that neither the President nor the VP thought that John was going to do it. In all truthfulness, neither did John. It was all a little surreal, just like the events of the whole day. Hell, he had been living in the surreal since all of this began.

The three of them watched the spectacle. The pink wig that the President wore was surprisingly fire resistant. After a couple of minutes, nothing was left but ashes and that pink wig.

Both the PRESIDENT and the VP died in terror and their screams put everyone else in the cramped room on edge.

John addressed the survivors.

"Anyone else feel the need to meet Jesus today?"

No one said anything.

"Ah, fuck it," John said, and burned them too.

OUTRO

Holden jumped, surprised, and exclaimed, "Why THE FUCK did you do that?"

John replied, "Those cocksuckers enabled this living hell. Fuck them. Let the country start again, from scratch. Maybe we can get it right this time."

"From the ashes, so to speak," said Austin. They all groaned.

They watched the bodies burn for some time, almost warming in the glow. It reminded John of his youth as a Boy Scout, when he had spent hours sitting around a campfire, telling ghost stories and enjoying the "great outdoors." A fitting end to these assholes, thought John. Burnt to a crisp, with not a single molecule remaining. Good riddance to bad rubbish.

The three of them looked at each other and without a word, walked out the door, up the stairs, and back into the main part of the building. The Presidential Palace was in disarray, littered with dead bodies and now on fire. There were cries from some of the wounded, but that didn't bother them. They were numb by now, caught up in the surreal nature of the experience. With the mission over and no one worth killing, they now wandered around, almost as if they were lost on a school field trip.

John looked at a painting of a man that he recognized as Abraham Lincoln. He thought of the man's legacy. Nearly two hundred years ago, America had fought a war over slavery, and this man had led the country through it, only to be murdered at the end of it all. He wondered how history would judge them. Would they be remembered as heroes or as terrorists?

"It depends on who writes the history books," John mumbled out loud, as if trying to speak to Abraham himself.

Austin looked again outside. Through one of the gaping holes in the walls he could see the massing of troops. While they had cut the head off the snake, the body of this evil empire was very much still alive and slithering. Thousands of SS Troopers, tanks, and vehicles had flooded the Presidential Palace grounds. Looking up, the sky buzzed black with helicopters. The sheer amount of enemy firepower should have made him want to shit his pants, but Austin felt strangely at peace. A warm sensation passed over him and he smiled. It was almost as if he could FEEL his wife and his daughter there with him. He knew he would be with them soon.

Austin said, "Let's go play outside."

"Why not?" John said, smiling. He had always loved that line from the movie *The Wild Bunch*. It sounded positively badass in this context.

Holden smiled. The feeling of hopeless optimism was contagious. "Let's go put these suits to the test."

They all laughed. It was going to be a long night.

9 798841 190875